Her smile sen **through him** **dangerous.**

Every nerve-ending screamed for him not to become involved. Bronte should leave. He needed her to leave.

But her determination swam around him, dragging him along. She planned to carve out a life for herself and her baby in a town far away from her own hometown.

Should he be forcing her away if she really didn't have anywhere to go? If her family didn't value her? If their love for the child came with conditions?

No, he couldn't send her back to a place where she wasn't valued or loved. No one deserved that. Everyone deserved a place to call home.

But the thought of her staying scared the hell out of him. He sighed, giving up all hope of having a doctor who could carry the heavy load needed, giving up all hope of the distance *he* desperately needed from this woman who invaded his thoughts and dreams.

Always an avid reader, **Fiona Lowe** decided to combine her love of romance with her interest in all things medical, so writing medical romance was an obvious choice! She lives in a seaside town in southern Australia, where she juggles writing, reading, working and raising two gorgeous sons with the support of her own real-life hero. Fiona would be delighted to hear from readers so please write to her at fional@ncable.net.au

PREGNANT ON ARRIVAL is Fiona Lowe's emotional, heart-rending debut novel for Mills & Boon® Medical Romance™!

PREGNANT ON ARRIVAL

BY
FIONA LOWE

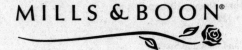

To Jude, Melissa, Serena and Nic:
inspirational women and critique partners extraordinaire.

First published in Great Britain 2006
Harlequin Mills & Boon Limited,
Eton House, 18-24 Paradise Road, Richmond, Surrey TW9 1SR

© Fiona Lowe 2006

ISBN 0 263 84745 4

Set in Times Roman 10½ on 12¼ pt
03-0706-45316

Printed and bound in Spain
by Litografia Rosés, S.A., Barcelona

CHAPTER ONE

BRONTE GRABBED THE handle of her suitcase and tugged. The old leather case stayed put on the trolley, refusing to budge. She tried again, this time pulling really hard.

The case moved quickly and suddenly, knocking her backwards. She found herself sprawled on the terminal floor, in a sea of assorted underwear and toiletries.

Great. Just great. It looked liked things were going true to form even though she was a thousand kilometres from home. She picked up some lacy underwear that had landed on her chest. The scattered clothes and broken case pretty much represented her life at the moment.

She stood up and hastily collected her belongings and shoved them back into the case as a few people looked on, amused.

'Dr Hawkins?'

A wave of embarrassment raced through her. *Oh, no, please no.* But she knew the score. This *would* be her new boss. And his first view of her had been with her bottom up in the air. She wanted to crawl inside the recalcitrant suitcase and hide.

Bronte glanced up very slowly from her kneeling

position. A pair of moleskin-clad legs came into view. Very long legs wearing workboots caked with red clay.

She followed his line of leg up across a broad chest to his face. Tanned brown by the outback sun, he had the tell-tale lines of a man in his thirties. High cheekbones defined a strong face, and the day-old stubble outlined a solid jaw.

Glossy magazine handsome he wasn't, but he had an attractive ruggedness about him. A man who lived life to the full. The type of man her sister dated. The type of man she now knew never dated her.

Except his sky-blue eyes seemed to be appreciating her behind. She must be imagining things. Travel fatigue must have got to her.

'Dr Morrison?' Bronte forced her voice to sound light and friendly rather than nervous and embarrassed. Without thinking she stuck out her hand to greet him, forgetting she was still kneeling.

His hand grasped hers firmly and a tingling sensation raced up her arm. He quickly pulled her to her feet, the strength of the pull propelling her straight into his chest. His very solid chest.

The warmth of his body mixed with hers. She stepped back quickly, heat flooding her face. 'Ah, sorry. Thank you.'

For a brief moment his lips widened into a grin, exposing straight, white teeth and he nodded. 'Yes, I'm Huon Morrison.' His gaze rested on Bronte, intense and vivid blue. Then his eyes flicked over the dilapidated case and he smiled. Dimples appeared, giving him a mischievous look.

Butterflies took flight in her stomach.

'By the looks of you and your case, this final leg of your trip to Muttawindi is about all you're both up to.'

'There's no hope for the case, but I'm fine.' She tried to smile but her face felt stiff. Why was her heart hammering? She was flustered, as well as giving the impression of being a total klutz.

She hauled in a calming breath. Time to take charge. After all, this was her new life. Taking in a deep breath, she flicked her head up, looked Dr Morrison straight in the face and noticed shadows of fatigue lingering under his eyes. The country had trouble attracting doctors and doctors already in the field worked long hours. Hopefully her arrival would ease his workload. And those shadows.

She forced her attention back to what she wanted to do. 'Please, call me Bronte.'

He took her proffered hand and shook it. This time his fingers wrapped around her hand gently, sending a delicious tingling along her arm.

'Welcome to the outback, Bronte. Call me Huon.' His fingers lingered for a moment on her hand. Warmth spread through her. Was he flirting with her? Men didn't usually flirt with a plain Jane like her, not unless they were trying to get closer to her gorgeous sister, Stephanie. It was a shame she'd taken so long to work that out.

Damien had been the last man to flirt with her and she was still dealing with the fallout from that disaster. Professionally she'd always stood up for herself. Outside work she didn't always have the same self-assurance. But the debacle with Damien had made her determined to transfer that work confidence into her personal life. She wouldn't allow herself to be used again.

She had no intention of dating again for a long time.

Unfortunately, that insight didn't stop the sensation of disappointment snaking through her when Huon finished the handshake.

'Muttawindi's been short a doctor for a while now, and we've been counting the days to your arrival.' He grinned again. 'It's great you're finally here and joining our community.'

She smiled back. His enthusiasm and welcome were infectious. 'I'm really looking forward to joining the team and settling in Muttawindi.'

'Excellent.' Huon picked up her case, securing it shut by splaying his first two fingers against the lid. With a businesslike sweep of his free arm, he indicated the double doors back to the tarmac. 'We need to leave now.'

She stifled a sigh. Definitely not flirting. Just her new boss welcoming his subordinate. Just good manners shining through.

'Follow me.' Huon strode off through the doors, out into the wall of heat, and headed towards a waiting plane.

Grabbing her handbag, Bronte ran to keep up with his long stride.

Halfway across the tarmac he turned and paused, waiting for her to catch up.

'Sorry to rush you, but we're taking advantage of the plane being free in between clinic runs. The workload's pretty steep out here, and we're often working against the clock, not to mention the heat.' His gaze raked over Bronte's petite body.

She recognised the analytical look that so many colleagues gave her, thinking she would not be physically up to the demands of medicine.

A spark of anger fizzed inside her.

For a moment his outback-blue eyes clouded with discomfort. 'You're very slight and this job is very physical.'

Bronte tossed her head back to hide the pain that always slugged her when people judged her by her physical appearance. 'Ah, looks can be deceiving, Doctor. I'm fit as a Mallee bull.'

'Good. You'll need to be.' He moved again towards the plane and at the steps he stood to the side. 'After you.'

The deep timbre of his voice sent a quiver through her and a tiny thrill flared at his courtesy. How could her body betray her like that? Had she learned nothing over the last two months? Couldn't her body work out that the man just had exceptional manners?

Huon ushered her up the steps into the plane and she ducked her head as she stepped inside. She looked around excitedly, pinching herself that she really was in a flying doctor's plane. Fitted out with two stretchers and a lot of medical equipment, the plane also had three normal passenger seats.

The pilot turned around from his controls as Bronte entered the plane.

'Bronte, I'd like you to meet Brendan, one of our pilots.' Huon's voice sounded in her ear over the dull roar of the engines, making her jump slightly.

'G'day, Bronte. Welcome to Broken Hill.' Brendan gave her a cheeky smile. 'Sorry I didn't come into the terminal but we're on a quick turn-around today.'

'That's OK, Brendan, I understand.' At least she'd only embarrassed herself in front of one man instead of two. She had to be thankful for that.

Brendan picked up his headphones. 'Huon will show you how to buckle up the harness and we'll get going. It's about thirty minutes to Muttawindi.' He smiled again and turned back to his controls.

'Sit here.' Huon directed her to a seat and pulled the harness over her shoulders, his fingers briefly brushing the tops of her arms. Warm tingles washed through her and she struggled to concentrate on his explanation of how the harness connected. But as she watched him click the buckle pieces together all she could think of was how his fingers had gently wrapped round her hand when they'd met.

Bronte wanted to shake herself. She was losing it. She didn't daydream about men and their hands. Especially a colleague's hands, her new boss's hands.

Time to focus and clear her head. This was the first day of her new job. Her new life. She leaned back in her seat and closed her eyes. She was tired, bone weary, in fact, which wasn't like her. But, then, with all the recent upheaval she had a right to be tired. Coming to Muttawindi was a complete change and a new start.

A new start she desperately needed after her foolish lapse of judgement. And a job that put a thousand kilometres between her and Damien. Thank goodness she'd never have to clap eyes on him again. Her cheeks blazed with embarrassed heat at the thought of her naïve stupidity. She'd believed every lie he'd told her and he'd reeled her in, then dumped her like a fish floundering on a pier. How could she have missed the warning signs?

This position was just what she needed. Muttawindi would give her a job she could sink her teeth into. A place where she could shine and be valued. A place to belong.

Now she just needed to make a good first impression in Muttawindi and wow Huon with her medical skills. Prove she had the stamina he thought she might lack.

She opened her eyes to find Huon scanning her face intensely.

'You OK? You look pale but your cheeks are fire-engine red. Do you have a temp?'

She forced her voice to sound light and cheerful. 'I'm fine.' Actually, she was feeling queasy but there was no way she was going to tell him that.

Huon buckled his harness. 'It's not far now. Muttawindi's only two hundred kilometres from Broken Hill. You'll soon see your new home.' His smile radiated hospitality and reaffirmed her decision to leave Melbourne and start again.

The engines roared and the King Air raced down the runway, quickly rising up into the cloudless sky. For a moment Broken Hill lay below them, defined by a seven-kilometre mullock heap. It quickly disappeared and the red dust of the outback, tied down with occasional clumps of saltbush, stretched out before them.

The throbbing sounds of the engine, combined with her fatigue, lulled Bronte into a relaxed state and her heavy eyelids drooped closed.

The plane hit an air pocket. Bronte's stomach lurched. Airsick? She'd never been motion-sick before, but she was definitely experiencing it now.

She pulled in a long, slow deep breath as another wave of nausea hit her. Bile scalded her throat. She gulped in air. She couldn't be sick, she wouldn't be sick.

'Are you *sure* you're all right?' Huon leaned over, concern etched on his face.

'I…I think I need…' Bronte's hands flew to her face as she began to heave. Huon quickly grabbed a sick bag and handed it to Bronte just in time for her to vomit. Mortified, the heat of her embarrassment scalded Bronte's cheeks. 'Oh, God, I'm so sorry.'

His body stiffened for a moment and then he relaxed and gave her a wry grin. 'Obviously you're not all right. Perhaps it was something you ate on the flight from Melbourne. Airline food can do that to you.' He reached out and grabbed a towel and a water bottle. 'Here, drink this.'

Bronte took a sip of water, trying to banish the acidic taste from her mouth. The pervading, acrid odour of vomit permeated the plane, making her feel ill again.

Vomiting in front of anyone was embarrassing enough, but chucking up in the company of her new boss wouldn't win anyone brownie points. 'I'm so sorry. I never get motion sickness. I don't understand.'

'Don't look so horrified. We're doctors, people vomit. It goes with the territory.'

Slowly, she leaned back in her seat. Another wave of nausea hit her.

'Here. Hold this.' Huon handed her another bag. 'We're going to start descending in a minute, which might stir things up again.' He gave her a penetrating look. 'And as soon as we're at the clinic, you're having a thorough check-up.'

She didn't have the energy to argue, she was too busy concentrating on not throwing up again.

The King Air touched down on the outback strip with a slight bump. As soon as the plane came to a halt Brendan released the door, and Bronte clambered out of the plane into the fresh but hot air, her hand gripping the stair rail. At first her legs seemed rubbery but they soon steadied and the nausea started to recede.

She glanced around. A low-roofed, utilitarian, rectangular building stood one hundred metres away with the obligatory rainwater tank standing at one end. A large, evaporative air-conditioning unit balanced on the roof, testimony to the oppressive summer heat of the outback.

'Come on inside the clinic, Bronte. You need to get out of this heat. Brendan will bring your bag.' Huon placed his hand gently under her elbow and propelled her forward.

His supportive hand at her elbow made her feel like a fraud. This wasn't the best way to start her new job. She was a colleague, not a patient. She stepped forward, away from his touch, putting a slight distance between them.

He opened the door for her. 'Have a seat in the waiting room.' Huon directed her to a row of moulded plastic chairs. 'I won't be long.' And he disappeared down a long corridor.

Feeling much better now she was on terra firma, Bronte didn't sit but took in her surroundings. Health promotion posters for Sunsmart and Quit Smoking programmes plastered the walls, many with peeling corners. The occasional piece of artwork hung haphazardly, interspersed with the posters.

Bronte noticed that all the artwork was original. She stepped closer to examine a couple of the paintings. Their colours reflected the outback perfectly—brown, orange, red and yellow with occasional flashes of green. They were good, worthy of their own display wall.

'Bronte, come on through.'

She turned from the painting to see Huon at the entrance to the long corridor. A white polo shirt with the clinic's logo and navy blue shorts had replaced his other clothes. The blue of his eyes and the tan of his skin seemed more vivid against the white shirt.

She swallowed and shook her head. She needed sleep and she needed food. Then she would be back to her old self, and her cast-iron stomach.

Bronte walked towards Huon. 'Look, I'm fine now. I think it was just fatigue. The last few weeks have been really hectic. All I need is a good sleep. So we can skip the check-up.'

'No, we can't.' He spoke firmly. 'You've looked peaky since Broken Hill. I need a doctor who is fit, well and on deck so let's just make sure you're not harbouring some nasty bug.'

'Really, Huon, I'm a doctor, too, and—'

'No arguments. I'm the doctor in charge and I'm pulling rank.' He ushered her into an examination room, sat her down and put a thermometer in her mouth.

She automatically rolled up her sleeve as he wrapped the blood-pressure cuff around her arm. She glanced at the sphygmomanometer as the mercury fell, feeling the blood pounding through her arm and working out a rough BP based on that.

'Fine,' Huon commented as he unwrapped the cuff, with the tell-tale sound of ripping Velcro. He removed the thermometer from her mouth and read it. 'Normal.'

'See? I said I was just tired.' Bronte went to stand up.

'Not so fast. I said a check-up so I need to test your urine.' He gave her a grin and handed her a small container. 'Why is it that doctors detest submitting themselves to a routine check-up?'

She threw him a look she hoped spelt out her displeasure at the process he seemed to find entertaining and stomped off to the bathroom. Fortunately, she was quickly able to fill the container. She didn't need any more embarrassing situations that day.

Returning to the office, she handed over her specimen. Huon took it over to a bench and stood with his back to her. She heard him unscrew a jar, which she assumed contained the Multistixs, to test the urine.

'Any headaches lately?' Huon walked back to his desk and sat down.

'No.'

He checked her eyes using his ophthalmoscope and then checked her ears with his auriscope.

'That's all fine as well.'

Bronte rolled her eyes. 'Just like I said, all I need is a good sleep.'

'Just humour me, Bronte. After all, I was the one who witnessed you being sick earlier.'

Heat burned her cheeks. 'Sorry about that. It's never happened before.'

Huon checked the lymph nodes in her neck and tapped her knees with his white plessor. 'No sign of infection so that's good. Perhaps your self-diagnosis was close to the mark.'

'Great. So now if I can just be taken to my house, I can get that catch-up sleep I really need.'

'I'll just check your urine test.' Huon stood up and walked back to the workbench. He checked the Multistix against the bottle's colour chart.

'All OK?' Bronte asked with a hint of self-righteousness. She noticed him pick up something else from the bench.

His shoulders stiffened and he turned slowly to face her. His smile had gone, his dimpled cheeks suddenly stark with tension. A deep furrow lined his brow and his expression was a mixture of disbelief and aggravation. 'You're pregnant.'

The two words hit her like a shot from a gun. The shock sent her blood rushing to her feet and her head swirled. This couldn't be.

Could not be.

She gripped the edge of the chair, struggling to think. She'd only slept with Damien twice and both times they'd used contraception. *The condom broke*. But she'd taken emergency contraception.

Oh, no! Surely she wasn't one of the twelve per cent of cases where it didn't work. Surely the gods wouldn't let that happen.

Huon pushed the white pregnancy stick into her hand. Two stark pink lines stared back at her.

Apparently they would.

'Oh, God.' She slumped in her chair and dropped her head into her hands. Of all the things she could have imagined happening to her, this wasn't one of them. This was not in her plan for her new life.

CHAPTER TWO

FRUSTRATION ALMOST MADE Huon vibrate. Bronte was pregnant. He couldn't believe it. When Head Office had rung him two weeks ago with the news they finally had a doctor to share his workload, he'd been sure his whoop of joy had been heard in the Barcoo. Now his plans of working with a colleague committed to Muttawindi for the long haul, and all the professional advantages that spun off from that, lay in a heap at his feet.

Why was it so hard to get a good doctor to come to the outback and stay? He was so tired of working alone. It had been a tough couple of years. After a string of locums they'd had 'Dr Disaster'. Muttawindi was still recovering from placing their trust in a man who had turned out to have fake medical qualifications.

How someone hadn't died in his care was a miracle, but his legacy had scarred and scared the people of the town. A new doctor was going to have to work really hard to regain their trust.

And he'd been convinced that the extra vigilance applied to the interview process and the quadruple checking of all the paperwork and referees would pay off. But now he had a pregnant doctor.

A pregnant doctor was just what he *didn't* need. Especially one that looked like a stiff breeze would blow her over.

Anger curled in his gut at her betrayal. By withholding this information she'd just snatched away his dream of some real help. 'I would have appreciated you telling me you were pregnant *before* you arrived. I would have told you not to bother coming.'

Bronte raised her head and looked at him, shock and bewilderment playing across her face. 'I had no idea I was pregnant.'

'Yeah, well, you do now.' His words sounded harsh and he regretted them the moment they'd left his mouth. Hell, she probably was telling the truth if the whiteness of her face was anything to go by. She looked as if she was about to faint. He pushed a glass of water over to her. 'Here, drink this.'

Her long, thick eyelashes caressed her cheeks as she blinked back tears. 'Thank you.'

A strange ripple of sensation flicked along his veins. He squashed the feeling immediately. Since Ellen's death his body had been dormant. He planned to keep it that way. The safe way.

She gripped the glass. Slowly a slight hint of colour returned to her face but she was still very pale. Determination sparked in her eyes, shards of blue shimmering across the grey. She pulled her shoulders back. 'This doesn't change anything. I'm still the doctor you need, Muttawindi needs.'

'Really? I need a doctor who doesn't vomit in a plane.' Sarcasm dripped off his tongue and his stomach clenched as the whole messy situation swirled in his gut. He let it take hold, pushing away the unsettling heat that had been part of him since he'd first seen her bent over that ridiculous excuse of a suitcase at the airport.

'You're pregnant—of course it's going to change things.' Aggravation made his voice rise. 'You won't even be able to commit to the full length of your contract. At best you'll be a temporary doctor, a fill-in. I don't need *another* locum. It's probably better that you don't even start.'

Pain and shock slashed her face, bringing him up short. Damn. He hadn't meant to be so blunt. He sat down next to her. 'Look, we've both had a shock but I think the best thing for you would be to head back to Melbourne, talk to the father of your baby and pick up your old job. At least you'll get maternity leave.'

'I don't want to go back to Melbourne. I—'

The radio crackled, drowning out her words. Mary Callahan's voice from the Broken Hill base sounded in the room. He turned away from Bronte's outraged face and picked up the handpiece. 'Huon Morrison at Muttawindi, Mary. What can I do for you? Over.'

Out of the corner of his eye he noticed Bronte move towards the radio, her expression serious and intense.

'Huon, there's been a fire at Gaadunga Station and a jackaroo is badly burnt. You're the closest doctor so Brendan is circling back to collect you. Over.'

'Right, Mary. I'll head out to the airstrip. Over.'

'Take Dr Hawkins with you. Over.'

'That won't be necessary, Mary.' He ignored Bronte's sharp intake of breath.

'Huon, there's no flight nurse on board so Dr Hawkins must attend with you. Brendan's ETA is three minutes. Over.'

His stomach churned. He had no choice. Without a flight nurse his hands were tied. Bronte Hawkins would have to come.

Well, she could have her one emergency run out of Muttawindi, just so she could see for herself the sort of work she'd be expected to do. The sort of work she was not physically capable of at the moment. It might just make her see sense. Then she, with her slate-grey eyes and lush mouth, would head south and he'd find himself another doctor.

But right now she looked like hell and he didn't need a sick doctor as well as a patient. He grabbed an unopened bag of jellybeans from his desk. He always had a stash for his young patients. 'Catch, Bronte.' He tossed the bag at her. 'Get some sugar into you, you're going to need it.'

The King Air's engines sounded. 'Let's go.' He ushered her out the door, back into the heat.

Fifteen minutes later Brendan's voice came through his headset. 'ETA ten minutes.'

Huon passed Bronte an intravenous set. 'Set this up, please, we're going to need a couple of lines.'

He checked the equipment. Burns cases were always unpredictable and he wanted everything organised. They'd have enough concerns with an unstable patient without equipment problems.

He glanced up to see Bronte efficiently priming two IV lines. The paleness of her face made her grey eyes seem even larger. She'd pulled her long chestnut hair back with a standard-issue rubber band, which made her look about sixteen. She had an aura of fragility that tugged at him.

He swallowed against the feeling. He didn't want his emotions tugged. He'd locked them down when Ellen had died and he didn't want them waking up now. Not ever. There was too much risk of pain down that road.

As the plane circled Gaadunga's airstrip, Bronte pointed to a ute tearing along the strip, a plume of dust raised behind it. 'What's he doing?'

''Roo run.'

'Pardon?'

'They scare off any kangaroos with the noise of the ute. We don't want to crash into a 'roo when we land.'

'Oh…right.' Her expression was a classic city-girl look.

The intercom crackled. 'Prepare to land, Huon.'

'Thanks, Brendan.' He nodded at Bronte as she buckled the harness correctly. Often it took a few tries before new staff managed it.

The landing on the baked dirt strip was straightforward with minimal bumps. Huon grabbed the resuscitation equipment and medical kits, which from the outside looked like fishing-tackle boxes. He passed one to Bronte.

They exited the plane into a wall of heat and a squad of flies.

Huon recognised Lachlan Phillips, the station manager, as he ran over to them, looking extremely worried.

'Doc, thank goodness. He's pretty bad.' He pointed to the very dusty Holden utility. 'I've got the ute.'

'Thanks, Lachlan.' Huon started to jog over to the ute. 'This is Dr Bronte Hawkins.'

Lachlan acknowledged Bronte with a bushman's silent nod of his head. He lent forward and took the resuscitation box from her. 'I'll grab that for you.'

'No, really, I'm fine,' Bronte protested.

'Pass it over, you'll run faster without it.'

She shrugged her shoulders as if in the presence of a foreign culture and handed over the large box. 'Thanks, Lachlan.'

The track down to the homestead had more potholes than road and Huon was worried how Bronte would cope with the rough track.

It was just another reminder that having her stay wouldn't work. He needed to worry about his patients, not his colleague. 'Hold on to the overhead handle so you don't bounce around too much.'

Bronte nodded and surreptitiously shoved several jellybeans into her mouth.

He turned away and looked at Lachlan. His brow was creased in concentration as he negotiated the track.

'So what happened, Lachlan?'

'Ben was priming the pump with diesel and, I dunno, there must have been a spark. The whole thing went up in a fireball.' His voice went very quiet. 'He's burned pretty bad.'

'What first-aid did he get?' Bronte leaned forward.

'We put him in the bath for a bit until he started to shiver and now he's on a bed with clean linen.'

'Well done. Cooling down a burn victim is the best thing you can do.' She gave Lachlan a warm, reassuring smile.

It was the first smile Huon had seen on her face since he'd met her. It totally changed her, lit her up, and the permanent slightly worried frown she wore disappeared.

His breath shuddered into his lungs. That smile could warm the protective ice he'd nurtured around his heart since Ellen's death.

The ute pulled up and they ran into the house. Ben, the jackaroo, lay on a bed surrounded by three very worried people.

'Come on, you lot, move out and give the docs some space.' Lachlan's voice echoed around the room.

'Hey, Ben.' Huon infused some lightness into his voice, knowing how scared Ben would be. 'How's it going?'

'I've been better, Doc.' The young man grimaced.

Miraculously his face was clear of any burns but his arms and torso were in a bad way.

'Pulse one hundred and twenty, resps forty.' Bronte pulled the stethoscope out of her ears.

He was reluctantly impressed. Bronte hadn't waited for him—she'd proactively taken a set of observations.

She pulled out the oxygen and unravelled the mask and green tubing. 'Ben, I'm Bronte and along with Huon we're going to get you stable and safely back to Broken Hill.' She touched Ben's cheek. 'I'm going to put this mask on you to help your breathing.'

Ben nodded and bit his lip. 'Can't feel me arms.'

Huon wanted to bite his own lip. Ben's black and yellow arms meant full-thickness burns. 'The burns on your arms are pretty deep, mate, which is why you can't feel them. We're going to put two drips into your legs so we can get some fluid into you. Your body will be going into shock.'

The station workers had done a good job of cutting off his clothing. Huon continued to examine Ben, using the rule of nines to work out what percentage burns he had sustained. With both of Ben's arms burned and his chest, he estimated he had burns to about thirty-six per cent of his body.

Bronte wrapped the blood-pressure cuff around Ben's leg to get a reading. 'Huon.'

The tone in her voice made him look up. A deep furrow marked her brow.

'BP is eighty-five on fifty.'

'Right, he needs fluids, *now*.' He opened up the medical bag and withdrew two large-bore cannulae. 'You put the drip in the left leg and I'll do the right.'

He rested his hand on Ben's leg. 'Ben, this is going to sting a bit.'

'Doc…it can't…hurt more…than my…chest.' Ben squeezed the words out.

Huon almost flinched for the young man. 'As soon as we get the drips in, we can give you something for the pain.'

Ben moved his head slightly as if a nod was too difficult. He closed his eyes, blocking out anything that would tax his preciously needed energy.

Bronte wrapped the tourniquet around Ben's calf and, using her fingers, deftly probed for a vein. 'Got one.'

Huon opened the cannula packet for her. She took it,

flicked off the plastic covering and cleanly inserted the silver needle into the vein.

'Well done.' He passed her the IV tubing and some tape. 'Open it up full tilt, we need to hydrate him stat.'

'Litre of saline and a litre of Hartmann's.' Her firm voice stated a fact rather than asked a question. Her actions so far demonstrated a doctor confident in her craft.

'Good idea. I'll put the Hartmann's up on my line.' He swabbed the other leg ready to insert the drip.

Bronte returned the favour of opening the packet and the drip went in quickly.

He was struck by how they anticipated each other. But this one example of her work wasn't enough to change his mind. He didn't need a pregnant doctor to worry about on top of all his other commitments.

'Thank goodness Ben's legs were spared or getting a drip into him would have been a nightmare,' he murmured to Bronte, taking advantage of the rare opportunity to share his thoughts with a colleague.

'Absolutely. But I'm worried about his breathing. Before we give him pethidine I'll recheck for stridor.'

He nodded. 'He could have an inhalation burn. Although the men did the right thing with the bath, I think he's hypothermic. We need to warm him up, but first let's get these burns covered.'

'Right. I'll check his air entry and you cover the burns?' She raised her brows as if requesting confirmation.

She'd worked calmly and solidly since arriving, working through the ABC of triage, not waiting for instructions like many new associates did. Her actions belied the fact that she felt unwell. He had to give her that.

Huon passed her the stethoscope. 'Go for it.'

He started to cover the burns with sterile non-stick dressings. He worked quickly, wanting to wrap Ben up in the space blanket as soon as possible. The medical mantra for burns sounded in his head—Airway, Breathing, Circulation, Disability and Exposure.

Bronte touched his arm and drew him aside. 'He's got a stridor that's getting worse. If we give him peth, that will compromise his breathing. But we can't have him in pain either, because that will exacerbate his shock.'

'Let's intubate him. I want him out of here a.s.a.p., but we need him stable for the flight. He needs to go to Adelaide, which is over an hour away.'

'So we tube him and sedate him. What about his hands?'

Bronte's question echoed Huon's own thoughts. The badly burnt, oedematous hands meant Ben's circulation could be impaired. He didn't need gangrene on top of burns.

'We'll watch them and do a fasciotomy if we need to.' Huon picked up the laryngoscope, the metal cool in his hands. 'How long since you last tubed a patient?'

'About a month ago.' Bronte met his gaze, her eyes almost saying, *Throw what you like at me, I'll catch it.*

'Right, then.' He passed over the laryngoscope. 'You're up and I'll assist.' He wanted to see how she handled the tricky procedure.

Bronte took in a deep breath, accepted the proffered equipment and walked over to Ben. Huon had to hand it to her. The only emotions being expressed were for their patient. Professional and empathetic.

Bronte touched Ben's cheek and his eyes fluttered open. 'Ben, remember when I told you we might need to put a tube in your throat to help you breathe?'

'Yeah, Doc, I do. Is it time?' His voice came out in a hoarse whisper.

'Yes, Ben, it's time.' She bit her lip at the stoic bushman's attitude.

Huon injected some pethidine into the IV bung. A minute later, Bronte inserted the 'scope, located the vocal cords and slid the number eight endotracheal tube down Ben's throat. She deftly attached the air-viva and began to squeeze the bag, providing the jackaroo with much-needed oxygen and bypassing his constricted trachea. She hadn't hesitated for a moment. She was completely up to speed with emergency medicine.

'Lachlan.' Huon called out for the station manager. 'Get Brendan to bring in the stretcher, we're almost ready.'

'What about catheterisation?' Bronte asked.

He smiled. This woman had all bases covered and pre-empted his thoughts. 'That's why we're almost ready. It's my last job before we evacuate.'

He quickly inserted the urinary catheter into the semi-conscious Ben. Brendan assisted with the space blanket and they soon had Ben loaded onto the back of the ute, the stretcher wedged into place.

Huon put his hand on Bronte's shoulder. He had to hand it to her—she'd been working like a Trojan for the last hour. But he'd noticed the surreptitious intake of jellybeans. She needed a break. 'This will be a rough trip. I'll take over the bagging.'

She threw him a scalding look, her grey eyes

flashing like glinting steel. 'I intubated him and I'm staying with him.'

'Fine.' Frustration threaded through the single word. Hell, he'd only been trying to help. He banged on the cab of the ute. 'Lachlan, let's get moving.'

'Right, Doc.' The ute moved forward, slowly negotiating the rutted road.

Huon breathed a sigh of relief when they arrived at the King Air. With skill born from years of practice, he and Brendan quickly loaded Ben safely into the plane, strapped him in securely and connected him to the ECG machine. Two minutes later they were airborne.

With Bronte caring for Ben, Huon entered the cockpit and radioed Flinders Medical Centre. He spoke with the burns registrar, giving a detailed history so the patient hand-over at the airport would be swift. Ben needed to be in Intensive Care with minimal delay.

He returned to the cabin and looked at Bronte. Her stethoscope framed her elfin face, and lines of exhaustion had etched themselves around her eyes.

Disappointment marched through him. This time Head Office had got it right. She was a real doctor, unlike 'Dr Disaster'. She was talented, good at her job and they worked well together. But already she looked dead on her feet. How would she be able to handle the workload Muttawindi demanded?

She leaned over Ben, adjusting his oxygen mask. Her skirt stretched tautly over her behind, outlining a delicious curve. His palm itched to touch it, his blood heating at the thought.

'How is he?' Focussing on their patient would surely make this unwanted desire go away.

'Stable.' Her grey eyes sought his. 'For now.'

He knew exactly what she meant. Burn victims could change in a heartbeat. Hell, it was good having a colleague to share those concerns.

'You worked well today.'

She looked at him incredulously, her eyes glinting. 'I'm a doctor. I did what I know.'

He sighed with frustration. 'Your competence isn't the issue. Muttawindi's needs and your pregnancy are the issues.'

'No, your stubbornness is the issue. I have a contract offering me a permanent position. Muttawindi needs another doctor, which is why I'm here.'

'Muttawindi needs a doctor who can cope with a punishing workload.'

Her eyes narrowed. 'I can do that. I've always worked long hours, they're not a problem to me.'

He sighed. 'Long hours might not have been a problem to you last month but right now you're grey with fatigue, you can't handle a day's travelling without vomiting and you've been mainlining jellybeans since we left the base.'

He ran his hands through his hair. 'How the hell will you cope? There's no one here to pick up the slack, unlike that big city hospital you've come from. And surely you'll want to be close to your family now you're pregnant.'

A slight tremor moved across her body but she remained silent, busying herself with checking Ben's observations. She recorded them on the chart.

Strained silence stretched between them but he knew the argument wasn't over. He could swear he could hear the cogs of her brain turning.

Suddenly, she reached into the medical kit and pulled out a mirror. She pushed it into his hand, her touch hot on his skin. 'Take a look at yourself. Those dark rings under your eyes speak volumes. You need a doctor to relieve some of your workload.'

Her voice was edged with steel. 'If you send me home now, you have no doctor. How long will it take you to get a replacement? Sounds like you've waited a long time already. I'm here, I'm ready to work and my contract's signed. You really can't stop me.'

Aggravation surged inside him and he ran his hand through his hair. Muttawindi deserved a good doctor and Bronte was that. But he needed real help himself. Not just a doctor for a few months.

He loved his job but being on call twenty-four hours a day, seven days a week was wearing him out. Life wasn't meant to be this hard. He'd lost Ellen. He at least deserved a break at getting work under control.

He had to see her make sense, make her see this wouldn't work. 'You realise you won't qualify for maternity leave?'

She nodded and bit her lip. 'I know that but I can promise you six months, perhaps a bit longer, and I can return to work when the baby is three months old.' She took in a deep breath, her small breasts straining against her crushed white blouse. 'Look, I didn't expect to be pregnant but you sending me away makes no sense. You need me.'

'Why are you so hell bent on staying?'

'Why are you so hell bent on sending me away?' Her gaze locked with his.

Because your smile does dangerous things to my heart.

Suddenly fatigue rocked through him. He was tired of doing this job on his own without the support of a colleague.

Bronte was here. Medically she knew her stuff. And the people of the district deserved the care of two doctors, no matter how short the time, no matter how disappointed they would be that yet another doctor wasn't staying for good.

He was over a barrel. She would have to stay even though it was a far from perfect situation. 'I can invoke the trial period clause.'

Her eye's widened in surprise. 'What's that?'

'Four weeks. You get to stay four weeks while I find a replacement.'

'Four weeks?' Bronte's tongue darted nervously along her lips, moistening them.

A deep longing crashed through him, heating his blood as he imagined her lips pressed against his own. He slammed the image out of his mind. 'It's my best offer.'

Bronte tossed her head defiantly. 'I'll be here longer than that.'

And the idea that she might terrified him.

CHAPTER THREE

BRONTE SAT ON the narrow, single bed in the sparsely decorated room at the Muttawindi pub. Flies and moths buzzed around the naked globe attracted to the feeble yellow light it emitted. Noise from the bar drifted up through the open window, which let in more insects than it did cool night air.

The red light from the cheap black digital clock read 11:00 p.m. Her first day in Muttawindi and she'd spent most of it traversing half of Australia. Ben was now safely in Adelaide. She and Huon had returned to Muttawindi only half an hour ago. With her belongings still in transit from Melbourne, Huon had insisted she stay at the pub.

The heat pressed in on her, making each breath an effort. She lay down, exhaustion permeating every fibre of her being. A slow trickle of tears slowly cooled her hot cheeks.

Pregnant.

She couldn't believe she was pregnant. Coming to Muttawindi was supposed to have been her new start. A time to put her past mistakes behind her, forget the pain of Damien, and to come out of the shadow of her sister. Establish herself as her own person. A baby had never been part of the plan.

Thoughts of babies had always been a long way in the future, coupled with the idea of a loving husband. What a joke that was. The conniving, duplicitous, horrible, biological father of this baby didn't know the meaning of love. He only knew self-interest.

The overhead fan turned slowly, moving the hot air across her skin. She rubbed her hand along her lower belly wondering at the life that existed there, growing daily.

One misguided mistake…

Now a new life was taking place.

She tried to get her head around that idea. She sniffed and shook her head against the pillow. Breathing slowly, she let her mind focus.

A baby would change her life. Well, she'd wanted change. Now she had it. More than she'd thought but change nonetheless.

Her baby.

Suddenly she knew her mistake had nothing to do with this baby. Her baby was innocent in all of this ugliness. It was a pure entity. One, she suddenly realised, she wanted. Desperately.

She'd come to Muttawindi to start again and to belong to a community. The baby, although unexpected, was an extension of that plan. Perhaps the baby would help? Babies crossed barriers that adults often couldn't. She'd always noticed how people spoke to pregnant women and new mothers, even if they didn't know them.

New place, new start, new life.

Going home to Melbourne jobless and pregnant

wasn't an option. Her parents had been furious when she'd announced she was heading to the outback. They'd expected her to become part of Stephanie's entourage now she was touring as a sell-out singer.

Bronte blew her nose. She would *not* fail at her first real step away from her family's unrealistic expectations.

She had four weeks to prove to Huon she could combine pregnancy and working for the flying doctors of Muttawindi. Four weeks to show him and the town she belonged, that she was committed and needed. Then Huon would have no choice but to keep her.

She rubbed her tummy again. 'Hey, baby, let's show Huon how determined we can be.'

'Morning, Marg.' Huon walked into the dining room of the Muttawindi Pub. 'Can you rustle up some fruit, yoghurt and toast, please?'

'Right-oh, love. But it's not like you to pass up my bacon and eggs.' The publican gave him a rueful look.

Huon laughed. 'It's not for me, it's for Dr Hawkins. I'll have your full catastrophe breakfast, seeing my coronary arteries have had a week to recover from your yummy bacon.'

'That's my boy. I'll serve it outside. 'Might as well eat it there before the heat drives you inside for the rest of the day.' She disappeared into the kitchen.

Huon looked around at the familiar paintings and sporting teams' trophies. He'd been coming in to see Marg since he'd been a confused and troubled fourteen-year-old, newly arrived in Muttawindi. Marg's kitchen was a favourite haunt.

Comfort food.

Even though Claire and Ron, his Muttawindi foster-parents, had been wonderful to him, visiting Marg had been something he'd treasured. Marg was like the auntie he'd never had. An adult he could talk to about all sorts of stuff. The stuff you didn't tell your foster-parents.

He loved her and he loved this town.

When Ellen had died, the town had been the only thing that had got him through that dark year of first experiences without her loving presence. He pushed the thought away.

Today he'd come to collect Bronte. He'd telephoned her ten minutes ago and a sleepy voice had answered. He sighed inwardly. She'd still be exhausted from yesterday.

Hell, he was. He hadn't slept much last night. His dreams had been filled with a pale face, chestnut hair and eyes that could change colour from grey to deep sapphire blue.

He'd given up trying to sleep. At five a.m. he'd been out for a stint on his road bike, pumping his pedals around, pushing the images of Bronte Hawkins out of his mind.

Dr Hawkins was a business associate. A very *short-term*, business associate. He had no plans to get to know her.

Getting involved with any woman, let alone a pregnant woman, wasn't on his agenda. He'd loved once and lost. He never intended to live through that nightmare again.

Besides, Muttawindi needed him, they depended on him. He'd let them down badly, allowing 'Dr Disaster' to practice. His gut churned at the havoc one crazy person had wrought on the town. He hated talking about it. He just wanted to put it behind him but the court case was still pending, waiting to bring the horror back in vivid memories.

He would never let this town down again. Nothing would distract him from that. Not even a pair of fine grey eyes.

Bronte pushed the pub's dining-room door open. She saw Huon staring into a cabinet of sporting trophies, his sun-streaked blond hair gleaming in a shaft of light.

Her stomach flipped. Surely that was the baby and the nausea. She could *not* be attracted to this man.

Her naïvety had led her to total disaster with Damien and she was never going down that road again. She'd had enough pain and humiliation to last her a lifetime.

Besides, she had a baby to consider and hadn't she learned in lectures at uni that men were not attracted to women who were pregnant with another man's child?

She tossed her head and stood up a bit straighter. She would not allow herself to be sidetracked by a crazy adolescent lust thing or whatever it was she had. She was a grown woman and grown women used common sense and ignored shimmering sensations that heated their blood for men they hardly knew. Damien had at least taught her that.

No, she needed to concentrate on her baby and her job.

She gave her cheeks a quick rub, wishing she'd thought to put on some blusher. She ran her hands down her very crushed blouse and linen shorts, legacy of having been in a suitcase for two days. *Honestly, Bronte, you could take more pride in your appearance*. She stomped on her mother's voice.

Somehow she never really felt comfortable in her clothes and had decided long ago that clothes were just a necessary item to keep warm. Or, in Muttawindi's case, keep cool. She sighed as she tugged at her blouse, which seemed to hang off her angular body.

How she'd coveted Stephanie's curves when she'd been a teenager. She gave an ironic laugh. In a few months' time she'd have those curves but not quite the way her teenage self had imagined.

She took in a deep, steadying breath. 'Good morning, Huon.'

He turned and smiled, dimples appearing in his cheeks for the briefest of moments.

Bronte bit her lip against the wave of heat his smile sent through her.

'Morning, Bronte.' His voice was brisk and business-like. 'I took a punt you wouldn't want a cooked breakfast, so Marg's bringing out fruit and toast.'

She gave him a wry smile. 'Gosh, how did you know?' The thought of anything else made her stomach heave.

'Lucky guess.' He opened the door to the outside dining area and ushered her through in front of him. The fresh scent of soap and peppermint tingled against her nostrils. She caught herself breathing in deeper, enjoying the crispness of his aftershave.

Concentrate!

She sat down, put a serviette on her knee and took a

delicate nibble from the toast, willing her reluctant stomach to accept it. She deliberately avoided looking at Huon's eggs and bacon.

'So I'm up for a full day at the clinic.' She matched his businesslike tone.

'Given your state of health, I think a half-day would be plenty.'

She looked straight back at him, forcing herself to concentrate on her words and not his amazing blue eyes. 'Yesterday you told me that Muttawindi needs a doctor who can handle a punishing workload. I plan to prove that I can.'

His hands stilled on his knife and fork, and the yolk of the egg trailed yellow across the plate. 'Bronte, when I said those words I was angry. You'd just arrived, had unexpectedly vomited and I was still reeling from the fact you were pregnant.' He sighed. 'When we get unexpected news, we're not always rational. I'm sorry. I don't expect you to kill yourself on the job.'

'I don't plan to. But I intend to pull my weight like any other doctor. After all, this baby will have to get used to his mother working, so it can start now.' Her voice cracked and she gulped down some tea. A baby. The thought still overwhelmed her. She gripped the mug, needing to stay in control. Huon must not see how vulnerable she really felt.

'Do you need some time off to sort out things with the father of the baby?' His air of concern almost undid her.

'No!' The vehemence behind the word ricocheted around the garden courtyard.

His lips curved upwards. 'Right, well, I can see you're vacillating on that point.'

She forced a half-smile. 'Sorry, that was a bit of an overreaction. The father and I…it was all a mistake.'

His face became serious. 'You're still in shock right now but the time will come when you'll need to talk to him. When you do, let me know, and we'll arrange for you to have a couple of days' leave.'

He reached over and for the briefest moment his fingers touched her hand. Then almost as quickly he pulled his hand back, as if he'd been scalded. He plunged his fork into his bacon.

The featherlike caress of his fingers stayed on her skin, warming her. *Remember his impeccable manners.* Of course, Huon's good manners had driven him to show some sympathy. His touch hadn't meant anything more than that.

She pulled herself together. 'Thank you, I'll keep that in mind.'

'And when you need to talk about the pregnancy, I'm a good listener.' Concern swirled in his eyes with an overshadowing of hesitancy. It was as if he thought he should offer to be a confidant but he didn't really want her to take him up on the offer.

She dragged in a fortifying breath. 'There's really nothing to talk about. I made a mistake, I'm pregnant, end of story.' She tried to sound brisk, matter-of-fact. Right now she couldn't trust herself to talk about the pregnancy, it was all too raw. And somehow he knew that.

Huon stood up. 'I'll just pay for breakfast.'

Bronte reached for her purse. 'Please, I'll pay for my own breakfast.' She didn't want to be beholden to him.

His eyes twinkled. 'Actually it's the clinic who's paying. All part of expenses for settling in new staff.'

Heat flooded her face. God, how stupid could she be? Of course he wouldn't be buying her breakfast. He was her boss. Would only ever be her boss. 'Oh, right, thanks…'

She turned and walked outside towards the four-wheel drive. She was such a social klutz. *He wasn't Damien.* She had to remember that. Remember that he had no ulterior motive and no reason to charm her. His only need was for a doctor.

Although she worried about convincing Huon, she felt confident of winning over the locals. She loved being a doctor and she knew she was good at her job. Her peer reviews were always glowing. It was only her family who failed to recognise her skills.

They hadn't been very enthusiastic when she'd entered medicine. They'd never really accepted that their two daughters were so very different with different talents and interests. Stephanie had succeeded in the celebrity culture, first as a model and now as a singer.

Her parents' focus had always been Steph, first as doting parents and now as her managers. Bronte had accepted long ago that her own achievements would never be valued in the same way.

But she took great pleasure in the knowledge that her colleagues valued her. She was an excellent doctor and patients found her easy to talk to. She knew she'd be just fine in Muttawindi.

She looked along the street. The morning sun was reflecting a fiery orange off the decorative iron verandas, emphasising the glory of the Victorian buildings.

The grand buildings left standing in the main street were testament to the wealth that had once flowed out of the soil. This was going to be her main street now. Bronte took in a deep breath, breathing in the scent of her new home.

Huon's long stride sounded behind her. 'Right to go?'

She ignored the frisson of sensation that skittered across her skin at the sound of his deep voice. Instead she nodded and swung up into the vehicle.

Watching him vigorously move the gear lever into reverse, she realised that Huon Morrison did most things with intensity and single-mindedness.

He reversed out onto the road. 'We have assigned you a vehicle for use while you're here, but it won't be arriving for a few days.' His voice was businesslike and brisk. 'For the next couple of days you'll be with me, observing, and you won't need a car. I'll give you a couple of days before I throw you in at the deep end.' He gave her a grin.

A grin that exposed deep dimples in his rugged cheeks. Dimples that took away the worn and tired look that seemed so much a part of him. Dimples that sent a river of tingling through her.

But she couldn't focus on his dimples.

She focussed on his words.

Huon continued. 'Everyone thinks the flying doctors' service is for medical emergencies and we do handle those, but most of our work is clinic based. As a sub-branch of the Broken Hill base we're an important link in servicing the people who live in the six hundred and forty thousand square kilometres that make up our area.'

Bronte had trouble imagining such vast distances.

Huon looked at her and laughed. 'I know, it's hard to visualise, especially when you've grown up in the city. But it was John Flynn's vision to put a "mantle of safety" across Australia. And between the twenty-one bases across Australia, we're doing it. No Australian is more than ninety minutes away from medical help.'

'That's something to be really proud of.' The fact she was now part of this organisation, and hopefully part of Muttawindi, gave her immense satisfaction.

'It is. But remote communities are still under-serviced compared with their city counterparts. Muttawindi only has a doctor now because of the gas fields that have opened up to the north. Before that, there was only a twice-weekly clinic.'

Huon turned into the clinic car park and pulled on the handbrake. 'Here we are.' His blue eyes had an intense, questioning look. 'I'm assuming your pregnancy is not something you want to announce just yet. Your secret's safe with me.'

'Thanks.' Her throat tightened. His consideration threatened to undo her.

Huon opened the door. 'Let me know if you get too tired, OK?'

His genuine concern washed up against her, battering her resolve to keep all her feelings about the pregnancy to herself. She was petrified that once she opened up she'd fall to pieces and reinforce everything he thought about her working here and being pregnant.

She forced a smile. 'I'll be fine. I might demolish your dry biscuit and jellybean supply, but I'll be fine.'

Excitement at starting her job bubbled inside her. Combined with her nausea, it felt quite strange. She followed Huon into the building.

An older woman in her fifties crossed the waiting room, looking straight at Huon, her smile of loving tenderness for him alone.

Bronte's heart gave a lurch. She wondered what it would be like to be loved like that.

The woman spoke. 'Huon, Dad needs you to ring him before eleven this morning. He needs to know what size tubes you need for your new bike.'

Bronte realised with a start that this woman in a nurse's uniform was Huon's mother.

Huon grinned and shook his head. 'I told him to write it down. Right-oh, I'll give him a call.' He paused for a moment and then indicated Bronte with an outstretched arm. 'Claire, I'd like you to meet Bronte Hawkins. Bronte, Claire is the practice nurse and my mother.'

Claire gave her a welcoming smile. 'Sorry about the bike-tyre thing. We generally try to keep family stuff out of the office but my husband's off to Broken Hill today and, as you can see, he's a bit forgetful.' Claire seized Bronte's hand and pumped it hard. 'Welcome to Muttawindi. I'm so glad you're here. There's enough work in this district for three doctors.'

The warmth of Claire's welcome enveloped Bronte.

'Pleased to meet you, Claire. I've been pretty excited about coming out here, too.'

Claire beamed. 'That's wonderful because after last year we need a doctor who wants to be here. Outback life is very different from what you've been used to in Melbourne, isn't it, Huon?'

'And that's why Bronte's on a four-week trial. To see if she, Muttawindi and the workload all match up.' Huon picked up a pile of patient histories as if to say, *Subject closed.*

Claire's open and welcoming expression suddenly changed, and a frown creased her forehead.

Bronte wanted to stamp her foot and yell, *It was his idea, not mine.*

'Well, let's get started, then.' Claire swept her hand around the half-empty waiting room. 'I was expecting more people to have come in today to meet you, but after yesterday's emergency greeting I guess you'll be happy with a quiet day.'

Claire turned to Huon. 'You take Bronte to the examination room, and I'll send the first patient down to you.' She turned back to Bronte. 'I'll give you a detailed orientation of the clinic later. Right now you can observe and get a feel for the place.'

Bronte had a feeling Huon was well organised by Claire and wondered how he handled working so closely with his mother. She turned to follow him but the older woman put her hand on Bronte's to detain her.

Claire dropped her voice. 'He works too hard. Even as a child he was hard on himself. Since Ellen died he's been driving himself into the ground. Huon needs a doctor who is committed to stay. The town needs a doctor committed to staying. They've had a rough ride recently.'

Brown eyes filled with the protective look only a mother could have bored into Bronte's face. 'This four-week trial was his idea, wasn't it? Silly boy, he's still whipping himself about…' She paused for a moment, reconsidering her words. 'You *are* planning on staying, aren't you?'

Huon had obviously not said anything to Claire about her pregnancy. Could she use this to her advantage? She had precious few allies at this point. 'Yes, absolutely, I plan to stay.' *Well, it wasn't a lie.*

'Good, because I'm not sure how much longer he can continue with his workload and still stay standing.' Claire had the look of a lioness defending a cub. 'So I'll be holding you to that promise.'

Bronte wondered again at the love Claire had for her son. She couldn't imagine her own parents protecting her in that way. She thought of the baby growing inside her and realised that she wanted to shield it from harm, like Claire wanted to shield Huon from exhaustion. 'I'll keep my promise.'

'Thank you.' Claire's looked softened. 'Off you go, then, and start your day.'

Bronte had the distinct impression of having been dismissed by the mother superior. Claire's words played around in her head. *Since Ellen died.* Who was Ellen? A patient, a child, a lover? Huon didn't wear a wedding ring. Curiosity clawed at her. She was desperate to know but knew she really couldn't ask. Not yet anyway.

Jack, the first patient of the morning, arrived in the consulting room a moment after Bronte. He looked to be in his eighties with a weather-beaten face. His gnarled hands rotated a worn Akubra hat by the brim.

He sat on the exam couch and gave Bronte a long, hard, scrutinising look. 'Does the girlie have to be here? She don't look old enough to be a doctor.' His gravelly voice rasped around the room.

'Dr Hawkins is a qualified doctor, Jack.' Huon's tone was all business.

'You sure this time, are you?' The old man's rheumy eyes sparked at Huon. He then turned their gaze onto Bronte. 'From the city, are ya?'

Bronte could feel the waves of his animosity crashing into her. Honesty was the only way to play this. She smiled. 'Yes, I am, Jack. City girl, born and bred.'

'The last three doctors were from the city. City people never last out here.' Jack spoke with the finality of a man who had seen a lot of life.

Bronte opened her mouth to speak, to tell him she was going to be the exception to the rule, but he turned away from her and back to Huon, as if dismissing her presence.

'I came about me flu injection. Seeing you threatened to jab me at the pub, I thought I better head down here.'

'Good to see you're showing some sense. You don't want to spend this winter in hospital, like last year.' Huon gave him a knowing look. 'As well as the flu injection, you'll need to have the pneumococcal pneumonia vaccine.'

Jack grunted.

'I'll take that as a yes. Roll up your sleeve.'

Huon took Jack's blood pressure and then organised and administered the two injections.

Jack stood up, rubbing his arm. 'Right, then. I'll be off.' He walked from the room without looking at Bronte.

Bronte felt like she'd been hit by a piece of four by two. Jack had blatantly ignored her. Not a sign of welcome had crossed his face. It was as if he didn't want her there at all. So much for fitting in.

Her chest tightened. She tried to fight the rising tide of anxiety. This wasn't the best start and the four-week clock was counting down.

CHAPTER FOUR

BRONTE SIGHED, PUT three black jellybeans into her mouth and chased them down with some ginger tea. They'd just returned from an early clinic run at the gas fields and she was grabbing a quick five-minute break.

It was hard to believe her first week in Muttawindi was over. How could seven days seem like a month? Nausea plagued her and some days she felt like she was wading through mud as fatigue clung to her.

She was living on a diet of dry biscuits and had dropped so much weight that her work skirts and blouses hung off her. They were less flattering than usual and she knew she looked like a very bony scarecrow.

It's hard to believe Stephanie's your sister. It's like comparing a swan to a plucked chicken. Damien's sarcastic words skated across her mind, trying to take hold, trying to bulldoze the emotional fences she'd erected against him.

She pulled in a deep breath, banishing his voice, and sipped at her tea. Ginger helped control the nausea and she'd bought out the small supermarket's supply of ginger beer and ginger tea. The young cashier had looked at her as if she had two heads. Buying condoms would have drawn less attention.

Her hopes of winning over the people of Muttawindi in a few days had turned to dust. Although they seemed friendly enough when she met them out in the street, it didn't seem to transfer across into the clinic. She'd imagined a steady stream of patients, especially women, knocking at her door, seeking her medical services. But that hadn't eventuated.

'Doctors! I've got a frantic mother on the line,' Claire's worried voice called out.

'Come on.' Huon stuck his head through the door and beckoned Bronte towards the communications room. 'You can take this call. It'll be good practice for you, and I can see how you handle a remote consultation.' He gave her a reassuring smile. 'Just pretend I'm not here and you'll be fine.'

Bronte followed, her stomach churning. She needed to get runs on the board so that the people in town would start to trust her. So Huon had no reason at all to send her away at the end of her four-week trial.

When she saw the array of electronics in the room her nerves stretched so taut they almost snapped. Claire's brief explanation of all the buttons earlier in the week fled her mind.

Huon gestured to a chair in front of a computer terminal and other electrical equipment. 'Sit down and I'll switch the phone over so you can use the microphone.'

She sat down harder than she'd intended. The office-chair wheels skated out behind her, and she gripped the desk to steady herself from landing on the floor. *Great start.*

Claire stuck her head around the door. 'It's Jenny Henderson. I'll bring in the history in a moment.'

'Thanks, Claire.' Huon slid over the remote station medicine chest's list of contents, a notepad and a pen. Then he flicked a couple of switches on the console. 'You're on.'

Bronte gripped the microphone. Apprehension pooled in her belly. 'Dr Bronte Hawkins speaking. What's the problem, Mrs Henderson?'

'Where's Huon?' The woman's voice rose in agitation. 'I need to speak to Huon.'

Bronte squared her shoulders. 'I can help you, Mrs. Henderson.'

'No…I trust Huon.'

How could she be part of this community if the people wouldn't trust her? Wouldn't let her help them, even talk to them?

Huon pulled the microphone towards him. 'Jenny, it's Huon. Dr Hawkins is going to do this call.'

'But you're supervising her, right?' Jenny's panic played down the line.

The pointed words hit Bronte in the chest. She pushed them down inside her. She was an experienced doctor, and an expectant mother. She needed this place to live and she would prove to this town that she could handle whatever they threw at her, one case at a time.

She took in a deep breath. 'Mrs Henderson, I want to help. Please, tell me what the problem is.'

'My son Mark's been playing out in the shed. Now

he's sounding a bit wheezy.' The anxiety of the woman's voice came down the line.

'Is he asthmatic?'

'No.'

'Is anyone in the family asthmatic?'

'His father's got mild asthma but it's under control.'

She wrote down 'Family history' on her pad. 'Could he have been exposed to any chemicals in the shed?'

There was a moment's silence. 'Only fertiliser.'

'Was he playing in it?' Bronte's mind raced forward, trying to work out what was happening. Not having the patient in front of her involved a certain amount of second-guessing.

Huon sat next to her with his arms across his chest, his body language saying, *This is your call, I'm not really here*. She had to handle this on her own.

Prove to both Huon and Jenny Henderson she could do it.

Jenny's voice rose in horror. 'Oh, God, he must have been. His clothes have a lot of white stuff on them.'

Claire handed Bronte the Henderson medical history. Bronte nodded her thanks.

'OK, Mrs Henderson—Jenny—take off all his clothes now.' If the child was having a reaction to the fertiliser, they needed to get him away from the particles.

She could hear the woman talking to her son. She drummed her fingers on the desk as she waited. Jenny's fear radiated down the line and the remoteness of outback life came home hard to Bronte. 'I've done that.' Jenny's voice trembled. 'But he's getting worse and he's gulping for air.'

'Get the spacer from the medical chest. It is a large plastic thing and it is number…' Bronte checked the soon-to-be familiar list in front of her.

'Doctor, I know the spacer. Now what?'

'Pick up the salbutamol blue puffer, number 107 in tray B. Puff one dose into the spacer. Then get Mark to put the spacer to his mouth and take four breaths. Repeat this three times until he has had four doses of the blue puffer.'

Bronte heard the phone clatter down as the terrified mother carried out the instructions. Bronte wasn't sure if she should wait and see if the boy improved, or put out a standby call for a pick-up. That sort of decision came with experience, and right now she felt very inexperienced. 'Huon, do I put in a standby call for a pick-up?'

'If I wasn't here, what would you do?'

'I'd put in a standby call.'

'Right, then ask Claire to do it.'

'I heard that. I'll contact Broken Hill now.' Claire's efficient voice trailed off as she walked from the room.

'Thanks, Claire.' Bronte turned her attention back to her patient. 'Jenny, is Mark's breathing getting easier?'

'Not really.' The mother's anxiety thundered down the phone to Bronte.

'OK.' Bronte tried to make her voice calm and soothing. 'We need to wait four minutes from the last puff and then we assess.'

She checked down the medical chest content's list and found the number for adrenaline. Mark might need an injection if he didn't respond to the bronchodilator.

Leaning forward, she gripped the microphone. 'Jenny, is Mark able to take deeper breaths now?'

'No! He's getting worse. His chest isn't taking in much air at all and his lips are purple.' Her voice rose in panic. 'What do I do?'

Bronte took a deep breath. 'You need to give Mark an injection. He's having a severe allergic reaction and we need to reverse that. I'll guide you through it step by step. How much does Mark weigh?'

'Um…about…twenty-five kilograms.'

Bronte did a quick calculation in her head. It was vital the correct amount of adrenaline was given.

'Take out the ampoule number 99. It will be in your fridge. Check the label says adrenaline.'

Bronte heard a rustling noise then Jenny's voice came down the line again. 'Got it.'

'Well done. Now, take the syringe out of the packet. Then snap the glass top off the adrenaline ampoule.'

As Jenny carried out the tasks, Bronte found the silence of the phone unnerving. She clamped her lips firmly, almost sucking them into her mouth, so she didn't talk again until Jenny came back on the line. It was important not to overwhelm the already panicked mother.

Once again the isolation of the rural community struck her. It wasn't just the patients who were on their own, the doctors were alone, too. Bronte was used to being in a large teaching hospital with colleagues to consult. Medically she knew what to do, but it was always reassuring to run ideas past someone. Huon didn't have that luxury.

She took a quick glance at him but his face was impassive. Impassive but exhausted. No wonder he looked worn out. It wasn't just the physical workload but the mental strain of doing this job all on your own.

The lines of fatigue were carved in deep around his eyes. Had some of the lines been added by grief for Ellen, whoever she was?

Jenny's voice came back on the line, sounding steadier. 'I've opened the syringe.'

'Great. Now push the plunger all the way into the syringe and take the cap off the needle.' She paused a moment to allow Jenny time to complete the task.

'Put the needle into the adrenaline and draw up the fluid until it gets to the marking of almost four.'

Again she paused. 'Ready?'

'Yes.' Jenny's voice wavered.

'Then hold the syringe up with the needle pointing to the ceiling. Gently push the plunger until the top of the black tip is level with three.' Hell, was that clear enough? Explaining something that she did every day without thinking was a big challenge.

'Doctor, I've got the stuff in at three. Now what?' Fear mixed with a stoic resignation in Jenny's voice.

'Swab Mark's tummy with the alcohol swab.' She heard Jenny's sharp intake of breath. 'Jenny, you can do this. Just remember that skin is tough so be quick and firm and the needle will glide in.'

Bronte rubbed her eyes. She wished she was right there with Jenny. Wished she could actually see Mark, hear his air entry.

Huon dealt with stuff like this every day. So could she. So *would* she.

A minute passed. 'Jenny are you there?'

'Yes, Doctor. I've given the injection but he's still having trouble breathing.'

'It will take a couple of minutes to work. Now repeat the puffer-in-the-spacer again. And then come back to me.' She turned to Claire. 'Mark needs to come to Broken Hill.'

'I'll patch you through to Base.' Claire turned to the radio to contact Broken Hill.

Another minute passed. 'Jenny, how is he doing now?'

'Oh, Doctor, he's breathing more easily.' Jenny's voice broke. 'I was so scared but the blueness around his lips has faded.'

Bronte let out a breath she hadn't known she'd been holding. She'd done it. She'd got through her first remote emergency. 'Well done, Jenny. Keep up the puffs.'

'Thanks, Doctor, I will. Now can I talk to Huon?'

Bronte's bubble of happiness burst. 'Yes, certainly.'

Huon leaned over in front of her towards the microphone, his hair almost tickling her face.

Bronte breathed in his mint-clean, wholesome, no-nonsense scent, which pretty much described the doctor beside her. She had an urge to run her hand through Huon's wavy hair.

Oh, God, what was happening to her? She was pregnant by another man, in a town that didn't trust her as a doctor, and attracted to her boss who didn't think she was physically able to handle the job. What would the psychologists make of that?

She pushed her chair back, putting much-needed space between her and Huon, and listened to him talk to Jenny.

'There's a plane at Wirriea Station, Jenny. They'll swing by and collect Mark in about twenty minutes.

Ring us back if you're worried about Mark between now and then.'

'Thanks, Huon.' Jenny hung up the phone.

Huon flicked off the microphone and turned to Bronte. 'You did well.' The deep resonance of his voice vibrated around her, making her heart skip. 'Handling a remote emergency can be scary stuff, especially when you don't have a colleague to bounce ideas off. And out here that is the rule rather than the exception.' His smile radiated understanding and empathy.

She looked straight into Huon's face, and tried hard not to let herself sink into those blue eyes that sparkled with shades of dark and light. 'But she didn't trust me.'

A slight frown creased his forehead. 'She got a surprise that it wasn't me, that's all.' Huon closed the medical folder in front of him. 'Come on, time for lunch.'

She followed him into the lunchroom feeling like a child that hadn't been heard. 'But it wasn't just Jenny Henderson. Jack didn't want to have anything to do with me either. Most of the patients I've seen this week have been disappointed I wasn't you. I thought country people were supposed to be friendly.' She heard her voice catch, and cursed herself for starting to breakdown in front of him.

Huon's face looked pensive and he ran his hand through his hair.

She remembered the last few times she'd seen him do that. It was when he didn't want to do or say something. 'So?' She prodded him for an answer.

'Bronte, this community's had a lot of doctors come through and stay for only a short time.'

'You're the one insisting on a four-week trial. I want to stay for longer.' Her voice rose in frustration. 'I don't plan to go.'

His eyes flickered with resignation. 'Look, when you took this job you weren't pregnant. I'm doing you a favour with the four-week trial so you know exactly what you're letting yourself in for workwise. Then you can make a truly informed decision.'

Frustration threaded through her. How did she get through to such a stubborn man that she'd made her decision already? She and the baby were committed to Muttawindi.

'How many doctors have been in Muttawindi in the last year?' She needed as much information as she could get to try and understand the town, understand their lack of trust.

'Four.'

'Four permanent position doctors have all left?' She tried to hide the incredulity from her voice, not able to believe the high figure. No wonder the town was slow to warm to her.

'Three were locums so they hadn't committed to stay.' He ran his hand through his hair in an agitated manner. 'The fourth one had to return to Sydney.'

His words came out harshly, surprising her with their intensity. But before she could comment, an awful thought thudded into her. 'Do the patients know I'm on a four-week trial?'

Huon looked affronted. 'No, of course not.'

'OK, so they're not biased against me because of that. So, how much time do you think it will take until they trust me?' She tried to keep the worry out of her voice.

'Word will be out soon on how you handled Ben's burns and how you treated Mark Henderson. The grapevine will start, but you can't rush it. Things take time.'

And that's what worried her. Time wasn't something she had a lot of.

Bronte found a note on her desk in Huon's barely legible scrawl. "Clinical meeting at twelve p.m., my office."

She glanced at her watch—it was almost noon.

The note surprised her. She'd had two weeks in Muttawindi and had worked out the routine of clinic life. But perhaps these meetings occurred on a monthly basis?

A clinical meeting usually meant case review. It seemed odd that he hadn't given her more warning or asked her to pull particular patient files to present.

She knocked on Huon's door and walked in. 'You wanted to see me?'

He looked up from his writing and smiled, his dimples briefly weaving their magic. 'I did. Close the door and grab a seat.' He moved a pile of medical journals from one of the chairs. 'My TBR pile.'

'Sorry?'

He grinned again. 'My to-be-read pile.'

She laughed to hide the swirl of heat that flooded her when he smiled, when his eyes sparkled a brighter blue. 'I've got one of those as well. They have a habit of multiplying when you turn your back.'

He casually leaned back in his chair. 'Have you read the latest clinic statement on antenatal care?'

She nodded. 'Yes, I did. I thought it covered all the pertinent points.'

'Great, so did I. So, let's get your blood tests organised.'

'What?' Surprise mixed with anxiety. What did this have to do with case review?

'You need to have your first official antenatal check-up. You weren't planning on doing it yourself, were you?' His gaze homed in on her face, reading her expression closely.

'No.' Defiance filled her and she met his gaze head-on. 'But with getting everything else organised I hadn't got around to arranging to go to Broken Hill.'

He gave a half-smile. 'Which is why I'm suggesting I take some blood and do the usual tests.'

Her anxiety took flight at everything involved in an antenatal check-up. 'I appreciate your concern but I'm your colleague, not your patient.'

He leaned forward, understanding dawning. 'I'm not talking a complete check-up, just the history, blood tests, BP and weight. Claire can help you with the rest.'

'Oh, right, of course…' Heat filled her face at his thoughtfulness, which she'd misunderstood again.

'The outback has its drawbacks and this is one of them. There's no other doctor for three hundred and fifty kilometres. As professionals we have to learn to compartmentalise our lives.' Kindness filled his voice. 'For fifteen minutes I have to be your doctor, not your boss, for the baby's sake.'

For the baby's sake. Of course he was right. She was being silly. She needed this check-up. It wasn't that she didn't trust *him*. She didn't trust herself. Her irrational attraction to Huon hadn't gone away like she'd hoped.

In the last week she'd found herself watching him, watching how the tendons in his hands moved when he examined a patient, how his eyes crinkled when he smiled, and how his biceps bulged when he assisted Brendan in loading a patient onto the plane.

And now she'd have to watch and feel his hands on her as he took blood. She dragged in a steadying breath.

Huon reached over, pulled out a history form and started going through the questions. 'What was the date of the start of your last normal menstrual cycle?

At least the first question was easy. 'December fifteenth.'

He spun the dial on the gestation calculator. 'September...'

'Twenty-first. I'm ten weeks.' She shrugged at his glance. 'I worked that out the first night.' He nodded in understanding. 'So, a spring baby. It's a good time of year to have a baby. He or she will be three months old before the summer heat kicks in.'

She gave a high-pitched laugh. 'Well, if you're going to have an unplanned pregnancy it should be at a convenient time, right?' She heard the quaver in her voice.

His empathetic look only made her feel worse.

'Any family history of significance?'

'Not on my side, no.'

He glanced at her, his eyes scanning her face. 'On the father's side?'

'I don't really know.' She bit her lip and swallowed. A wave of emotion rolled in on her, threatening to swamp her. For two weeks she'd avoided talking about the pregnancy. Avoided talking about Damien.

Tears pricked at the backs of her eyes. The doctor in her knew that holding on to grief and pain only made it worse, but she'd held on to it because she didn't want Huon to know how stupid and naïve she'd been.

She didn't want anything to damage her chances of staying in Muttawindi. She only wanted him to see the competent doctor, the professional who was on top of things and in control. She wanted him to realise she was the doctor he could rely on to work with him in Muttawindi for a long time.

So she'd said nothing, kept her own counsel.

But his gentle, caring approach had brought all her feelings rushing to the surface, and she couldn't hold them in any longer.

Telling him meant exposing herself to his scrutiny, risking everything. But despite what he might think of her, despite the danger he might not think her worthy of staying, she had to take the risk of telling him the whole sordid story. She couldn't hold on to it any longer.

Huon watched the colour drain from Bronte's face. She looked as fragile as a porcelain doll, as if one knock would shatter her.

He must have pushed her too hard this morning at the busy gas fields' clinic. Damn. Guilt trailed through him at scheduling this meeting at lunchtime. He might be able to keep going but Bronte needed to have regular meals.

He pulled over a platter of sandwiches Claire had made for them. 'You look really pale—eat a sandwich.'

He passed the platter of food towards her. 'Tuna's good for the baby.' He gave her a wry smile.

She failed to meet his gaze.

The guilt dug in deeper.

Bronte constantly looked like she was going to faint. *That* was the reason he knew she needed to be reassigned to another base. She didn't have the stamina for Muttawindi. Right now she was putting on a brave front, almost ignoring the pregnancy. But sooner rather than later, reality would hit her. Hopefully by then he would have a replacement doctor and she would be back in Melbourne with the father of her baby and her family.

He watched her nibble her sandwich. She'd lost weight since she'd arrived. The only thing plump about her was her lips. And images of those lush lips on his skin haunted his dreams every night.

And *that* was the most important reason she had to leave Muttawindi. If she weren't here, she wouldn't invade his thoughts. Couldn't unsettle the solo life he'd made for himself since Ellen had died.

He tried to call up the image of Ellen's face, but the shadowy likeness, now indistinct, hovered for a moment then faded. He'd adored Ellen. She'd been his first love. Now he could hardly picture her.

His heart contracted in a familiar pain. The pain some days he thought he controlled. Death had stolen Ellen's life, and he'd accepted that. But now time had stolen her image. He hated that.

The quietness of Bronte's voice sliced into him, dragging him back to the present. 'I only knew the father of the baby for a few short weeks.' Tension emanated from rigid shoulders. She put the sandwich down and clenched her hands into tight balls. Her whole demeanour spoke of a person at battle with herself.

'Some people might call it a brief affair. I don't know if it even qualifies as an affair. I foolishly thought it was love and the beginning of a future together.'

'Love can blind us.' Huon's words sounded trite against the pain in her voice.

Bronte shuddered. 'Well, it sure did that to me. I made a monumental mistake. I was really, really stupid.' Her voice quavered for a moment before becoming firm. 'My sister is Stephanie Hawkins.' Her gaze met his directly, as if expecting some kind of reaction.

The name rang a distant bell. 'Is she the actress that's now a singer? Sorry, I'm not that up with celebrity gossip.'

She gave him an ironic look. 'That's one of the things I love about Muttawindi. It's a long way from the high life.'

'Hey, we've got the B and S balls.' His eyes twinkled in mock defence. 'But you're right, it's a far cry from the Crown Ballroom.'

She dragged in a deep breath. 'Yes, Stephanie is the singer and her latest album just went platinum. She's also the face of Maybar make-up.'

So that was where he knew the name. 'I think I've seen her in one of Claire's magazines. That's pretty big in the celebrity stakes.'

She nodded. 'It is. And Steph's worked really hard to get where she is.'

'As have you. Passing your medical exams is no walk in the park.' He gave her a smile, hoping it would relax her. The doctor in him knew she needed to talk. She'd effectively avoided it for two weeks.

But the man in him didn't want to be her confessor. The less he knew about her the better. But he couldn't stand to see her upset.

'Thanks, but in the eyes of my parents it fades compared with stardom.' She bit her lip. 'My parents expected the whole family to be part of Steph's business, and up to a point I'd gone along with that.'

'Family's a strong pull.' Huon focussed on reflecting her thoughts back to her, counselling style. A counsellor was objective. A counsellor didn't get involved. A counsellor didn't see the person on the other side of the table as a beautiful woman with eyes that made his body throb.

'It is, but I'm twenty-eight and it's time for me to carve out my own life. I met Damien at the time I was convincing my parents I needed to leave the family firm and not be part of Steph's entourage.'

She gave a wry smile. 'He made me feel special. He did the full-on seduction thing. He'd text me at work, send me flowers, wine and dine me.' Her grey eyes suddenly flashed silver. 'And in a superb piece of acting that completely fooled me, he really seemed to understand where I was coming from and what was important to me.'

She sighed. 'But conmen work out your weaknesses, don't they? Unlike the family, he supported me in my plans. He even talked of coming to the outback with me. For the first time in my life I had an idea of what it must be like to be my sister.' She nibbled her bottom lip.

The unconscious action sent a wave of longing

through Huon. A familiar longing. One that had arrived the day Bronte had. It would go when she left in a couple of weeks. It had to.

Right now he had to concentrate on being a counsellor. 'We all love to feel special. There's no crime in that.'

'No, there isn't, but when reality breaks through the fog of what you thought was love, the actions of the other person can seem like a crime.' Bitterness tinged her words. Her hands were still curled into tight fists.

He wanted to lean forward and touch her, comfort her. But he leaned back instead, needing all the space between them that he could get. 'So what did Damien do?'

Pain slashed her face, the muscles tightening as her memories came back. 'On the night of Steph's Maybar launch at the Crown Ballroom, Damien had left his laptop at my place. He rang, needing an advertising file for a client, and asked me to print it off for him and bring it to the ball.

'I found the file but I also found his screensaver. It was a raunchy picture of Stephanie. He also had an enormous folder filled with hundreds of photos and articles about her.'

Huon forced his thoughts onto Bronte's words rather than her. If he focussed on her pain, he'd lose his objectivity. 'That must have been a huge shock. What did you do?'

'I arrived at the ball ready to confront him, and saw him at the bar deep in conversation with a friend. They had no idea I'd arrived and I overheard Damien talking about "Operation Stephanie". Apparently his plans were coming along really well, even though he had to put up with spending time with the unattractive sister to get closer to Steph. Every dull minute spent with me would be worth it when he landed the famous Stephanie Hawkins in his bed.'

Anger curled in Huon's belly. He wanted to physically thump the guy that had caused Bronte so much anguish. But all he could do was try and make her feel a little better. 'Ouch. So this guy is a complete bastard?'

Her eyes filled with gratitude and she smiled, her strength radiating through her pain. 'Absolutely. I'm better off without him.' She tossed her head. 'I slapped him so hard he fell off the barstool. I hope his physio bills hurt him just as much as his bruised coccyx.'

A wicked grin crossed her face as she met his gaze, her eyes taking on a smoky hue. A flare of heat ripped through him, blasting its way into the deepest spaces of his body. Defrosting the cold that had seeped into him since Ellen's death.

Scaring him.

The counsellor kicked back in, taking control. 'Does Damien know about the baby?'

The smoky hue in her eyes disappeared instantly, replaced by glinting slate. 'No. We used contraception so it's going to be a shock.' A frown creased her forehead. 'I'll tell him when I'm ready to deal with communicating with him. I don't want anything to do with him but he deserves to know a baby exists.'

He admired her attitude. Telling him wouldn't be easy. 'What about your parents?'

Her mouth tightened and she stared him down. 'When I'm settled in Muttawindi, when my job here is confirmed and I'm further along in the pregnancy, then I'll tell them. That way it's all a *fait accompli* and they have *no choice* but to respect my decision. If I told my parents now, they'd just try and organise me and take over.'

He needed to be devil's advocate, that's what a counsellor did. 'Grandparents usually want their grandchildren close by.'

She breathed in deeply. 'Haven't you heard what I've been saying? I have to make a break from my family. Their brand of love comes with many conditions and it is suffocating. It took me twenty-eight years to work out that no matter how hard I worked I would never be as special as my sister. I am *not* subjecting my child to that.'

Huon ached inside for this baby who would be denied a family. He'd been there and it hurt like hell. All kids needed a family.

'But—'

Her voice cut across his. 'I plan to bring the baby up by myself. I want this baby to be raised surrounded by love, not disappointment.'

Her point rammed home. He knew only too well that a kid needed unconditional love to grow and flourish. Muttawindi had given it to him when he'd arrived homeless and alone. 'It's not going to be easy for you, raising this child alone.'

'No. But then again, most things worth doing aren't easy.' She gave him a tired smile.

A smile that sent a jolt of desire through him. Electric and dangerous.

Every nerve ending screamed for him not to become involved. She should leave. He needed her to leave.

But Bronte's determination swam around him, dragging him along. She wouldn't waver in the face of his arguments. She planned to carve out a life for herself and her baby in a town far away from her own home town.

Should he be forcing her away if she really didn't have anywhere to go? If her family didn't value her? If their love for the child came with conditions? An image of a lonely boy desperate for love flooded his mind.

No, he couldn't send her back. Couldn't send her and her baby back to a place where they weren't valued or loved. No one deserved that. Everyone deserved a place to call home. And Muttawindi loved a stray. He knew that only too well. As soon as they realised what a great doctor she was they'd embrace her and the baby. Could he deny her and her child what the town had given him?

But the thought of her staying scared the hell out of him. In two weeks she'd caused him to experience sensations he'd forgotten he could ever feel. Sensations he knew would only lead to more pain. Life had taught him that.

But he couldn't send her back and still have a clear conscience. He sighed, giving up all hope of having a doctor who could carry the heavy load of Muttawindi, giving up all hope of the distance *he* desperately needed from this woman who invaded his thoughts and dreams.

He ran his hand through his hair in resignation. 'You're determined to stay, so go ahead.'

Disbelief raced across her face, quickly followed by relief. 'You won't regret this decision.'

But he already did.

CHAPTER FIVE

BRONTE SQUEEZED A Muttawindi-grown lemon into a glass of cool, spring water. She drank it quickly, quenching a thirst generated by two hours of non-stop talking on the radio clinic.

It had been three weeks since Huon had dropped the issue of a trial period and she'd thrown herself into work. She'd been putting in long days, needing to prove to Huon that he'd made the right decision. And she'd been trying to connect with Muttawindi.

It had taken a *lot* of convincing but he'd finally taken a Saturday morning off, leaving her in charge. It seemed strange to be alone. Part of her missed seeing his rugged, tanned face, the determined set of his jaw and the blond cowlick that refused to be tamed.

The sensible part of her knew a day away from him would give her much-needed breathing space from her growing attraction.

But even though he wasn't in the clinic, his presence seemed everywhere. Visions of his sparkling eyes, crinkling at the edges when he smiled, filled her mind. She could hear his deep, melodious laugh when she closed her eyes and see his passion for his town and patients.

Everyone in the town adored him. It hadn't taken long to work that out. Everyone spoke of him in glowing terms. But no one had mentioned Ellen. She desperately wanted to know who she was but knew she had no right to ask. Yet.

Work. She needed to think about work.

Work was what she needed. Work kept her focus off Huon.

She rubbed her tummy. 'We did OK this morning, you and me. People are starting to warm to us.' She'd taken up chatting to the baby—it sort of helped the whole pregnancy thing seem more real.

But she wanted to be much more than second best to Huon. She bit into a dry biscuit. He tended to hover over her like a mother hen, double-checking everything. It didn't help the town get to know her and she needed time alone with this community as a doctor. Bonding time.

She was certain the more they saw her in action, the more they would accept her. And this morning's clinic had been a building block. Although the town wasn't throwing a ticker-tape parade for her, this morning had been a solid start.

The radio sounded. Bronte pressed the microphone to 'on'. 'Dr Hawkins at Muttawindi, Mary. Over.'

'Dr Hawkins, we've had a call from Greg Tigani, the manager of the citrus orchard out on the Kintawalla Road. He's bringing in his two-year-old son by car. ETA five minutes. Over.'

'Any information? Over.'

'Sorry, Bronte. Greg's mobile went out of range.'

'OK. I'll be on standby. Over and out.' She walked over to the treatment room and checked the oxygen and suction. Claire kept everything in working order but it was always good to check.

The toddler probably had a high temperature. The current viral illness going around had kids spiking high fevers all over town.

Well, she could reassure the dad, and hopefully send away another happy customer who would spread the word that Bronte Hawkins was OK. Every case helped her cause.

She heard the wire door slam and she ran down the corridor. A very worried-looking man in workboots, shorts and T-shirt cradled a toddler in his arms.

'I need to see the doc.' The man's voice wavered.

'I'm the doctor, the new doctor—Bronte Hawkins.' She gave the man what she hoped was a reassuring smile. 'Please, bring the little guy down here.' She walked down the corridor and ushered the man into the treatment room.

'What's his name?' Bronte indicated a chair for the man to sit down.

'Tom. He's Tom and I'm Greg. Greg Tigani.'

'Pleased to meet you, Greg. What's been happening with Tom?' Bronte looked at the pale little boy who was snuggled into his dad's chest.

'He hasn't been quite himself the last day or so.'

'Has he had a temperature?'

'Maybe, but not really high. We haven't actually

taken it. But he got worse on the trip in. I think he's been having some sort of fit. He can't seem to swallow properly or open his mouth. Can you help him?'

'I'll certainly do my best.' The history medical of illness was confusing, with nothing really specific to go on. Kids with fevers were prone to febrile convulsions so perhaps he'd fitted in the car.

Except he was cool now. 'Greg, I need to examine Tom, so if you lay him on the examination couch you can sit next to him and hold his hand.'

The little boy's pale face was almost whiter than the sheet underneath him. The child was awake, not drowsy. If he'd fitted in the car, he should have been drowsy.

'Doc, I thought you'd have finished for the day. I was that worried I wouldn't be able to find you.'

Bronte looked at the troubled father's face. 'Running late has its advantages.' She put her hand on his arm for a moment to support him. 'I'm glad I'm here.'

'Me, too, Doc. Me, too.' Greg's heartfelt words gave Bronte a buzz of happiness.

She bobbed down so she was at the same level as Tom and gave him a smile. 'Hi, Tom, my name's Bronte and I'm going to have a look at you and try and make you better.'

Tom gripped his dad's hand and whimpered.

As Bronte reached for her stethoscope she heard the wire door slam with its usual bang, and footsteps sounded in the corridor.

'Hello, Greg, Bronte.' Huon walked through the door, nodding to both of them.

Surprise raced through Bronte. What on earth was he

doing here on his day off? Couldn't the man stay away from the clinic for one full day?

'Huon, Tom's crook. Can you have a look at him?' Greg's voice cut across Bronte's thoughts.

What? A wave of resentment mixed with disappointment surged inside her. A moment ago she'd been Tom's doctor. Now, with Huon here, Greg seemed to be dismissing her. What was Huon trying to do to her? Undermine her?

'Dr Hawkins is examining him, Greg, but I can stay if you like.' Huon came over to Tom and tousled his hair.

Bronte tamped down her anger. Huon wasn't taking over. He'd acknowledged her as the primary doctor, but his arrival meant Greg would naturally turn to the doctor he'd known the longest.

Bronte pulled her mind back to her patient. Tom needed her complete attention. Placing the stethoscope on Tom's chest, she listened carefully. The toddler's heart rate was slightly elevated, but air entry to his lungs was clear.

'Greg, you said that Tom had been unwell for a couple of days?' Bronte asked her question to Greg's back as he was looking at Huon.

'Sort of, but not really. Last night he didn't want to eat dinner. He's had times when he cries like he's in pain. And at breakfast Nancy tried to get him to eat and he wouldn't. It's like he wants to talk but sometimes he can't.' Greg's large frame seemed to slump with worry. 'Huon, what do you think is wrong with him?'

'That's what Dr Hawkins and I are going to work out.' Huon turned to Bronte, his face worried.

He had a right to be worried. So far Tom's symptoms

were so vague she didn't have a clue what was wrong, but the child looked seriously unwell. 'Has he been sick in the last couple of weeks and then got better?'

'No.' Greg shook his head. 'The other kids got summer colds but he's been fit as a flea. Can't keep him inside—he's always off climbing something.'

'Can you open your mouth wide like this, Tom?' Bronte made a large O with her mouth.

The little boy copied her.

'Oh, mate, you didn't do that for Mum at breakfast.' Greg turned to Huon. 'He wasn't able to do that in the car either. I don't understand.'

Huon ran his hand across his jaw. 'When he couldn't open his mouth, was his body rigid, like a spasm?'

'Yeah.' Greg nodded. 'Like his muscles all went tight.'

Bronte looked at Huon and a thread of understanding ran between them. She quickly and closely examined Tom's arms and legs. On the base of Tom's foot she found a sticky plaster.

'When did Tom cut his foot, Greg?' Bronte couldn't disguise the urgency in her voice.

'Not sure. A week ago probably.' Greg turned to Huon, deliberately blocking Bronte. 'Look, I didn't come here about a small cut on the foot.'

Bronte quickly pulled on the beige edges of the dressing, removing it to expose a small cut with a moderate amount of pus.

'Huon.' Bronte pointed to Tom's foot.

She watched Huon's eyes darken with frustration and resignation on seeing the cut. She sensed an amazing connection with him. It was like they shared a network link. They'd built on each other's knowledge and had come to the same diagnosis. 'Greg, are Tom's immunisations up to date?'

'Immunisations?' Greg looked confused for a moment.

'His vaccinations for tetanus, diphtheria and whooping cough—are they up to date?'

Greg's face cleared. 'Nancy read an article about brain damage, so we decided not to get him jabbed.' He turned away from Bronte. 'Huon, you know how we feel about this. Can you just focus on Tom rather than asking me stuff that's got nothing to do with him being sick?'

Huon spoke, his voice tightly controlled. 'Greg, this is the very reason I've pushed for you to immunise the kids.'

The lights flickered and a spasm contorted Tom's body. The little boy's jaw went rigid and the muscles of his face pulled up, giving him a grinning expression.

'Hell—trismus.' Huon grabbed the intravenous set. 'Get the magnesium sulphate, Bronte. We'll run it in through an IV to manage the spasms.' He turned to Greg. 'Tom's got tetanus. When he has a spasm he can't open his mouth. Lockjaw is an early sign.'

Greg put his head in his hands. 'Tetanus! But how can he…?'

Bronte wrapped the tourniquet around Tom's arm and found a vein for the IV. 'Greg, tetanus spores are found in manured soil and they will grow in any wound. It can be a clean wound or a deep, mucky wound. The spores are happy in either. Tom loves being outside and like most kids he probably runs around in bare feet.'

Greg raised his head, desperation clawing at his face. He looked at them both. 'Is he going to be all right?'

Bronte shared a fleeting look with Huon. Neither of them knew. 'He needs to go to Adelaide. He needs to have human tetanus immunoglobulin, which is only available in major cities. He'll be nursed in Intensive Care and he might need to be ventilated—have a machine breathe for him—if the spasms get really severe.'

Huon placed a clear paediatric mask on Tom's small face to give him extra oxygen. 'Bronte's right. Tom needs to go to Adelaide. Right now we're going to sedate him to help reduce the spasms, along with the other medication we're giving him.'

'Can Nancy or I go with him?'

Huon put his hand on Greg's shoulder. 'Of course you can, but timewise it will probably be you. Ring Nancy from the phone at Reception.'

Greg stood up slowly, kissed Tom on the forehead and headed towards the door.

Huon turned to follow. 'I'll call Base and organise the flight.'

Bronte nodded and glanced down at Tom, watching the rise and fall of his chest. He was spasm free now, but for how long? It was the first case of tetanus she'd ever seen and she had no idea exactly how the disease would play out.

He was a desperately ill little boy and she couldn't wait to get him to Adelaide. The trip could be a nightmare as Tom could fit again at any moment. She and the flight nurse would have to be vigilant in their observations.

Huon walked back into the room, his expression less dark than when he'd left. 'We're in luck. Brendan can be here in five minutes.'

'Thank goodness something's working out for Tom. Who's the flight nurse?'

'It should be Hayley, which is great as she's got loads of paediatric experience. Mind you, none of us have much experience with tetanus. This is only the second case I've ever seen.'

He tilted his head and the sunlight glinted off his blond hair in a halo effect. He smiled. 'You did well to diagnose it. I'm impressed.'

'Thank you.' Warmth rushed through her at his compliment. Warmth combined with the deep longing that his smile always evoked. A smile that always made her feel so very special.

Which was ridiculous because he smiled at everyone that way. She had no reason to feel more special than anyone else.

Bronte pulled her mind back to her patient. She adjusted Tom's IV. 'I'll be happier when he's in Intensive Care.'

'Me, too.'

Greg walked back into the room. 'I just heard the plane. Nancy won't make it in but she's organising to come to Adelaide on a flight out of Broken Hill tonight. She's getting onto her mum to mind the other kids.'

'Right. Well, she can ring Bronte for regular updates.' Huon scooped up Tom. 'Grab the IV, Bronte.'

Bronte disengaged the IV from the pole and they slowly walked out to the airstrip with Greg in tow.

Brendan had left the plane's engines running while he opened the plane door. As Huon's foot hit the bottom step he yelled out to Bronte, 'Give the IV to Greg, it will be faster that way.'

'What?' She could hardly hear her own voice over the engine noise. She had no idea what Huon was talking about.

'I'll give you an update when we get to Adelaide.' Huon nodded to Greg. 'Come on.'

Bronte's brain stalled. Tom was *her* patient. She should be on that plane with Tom and Greg, not Huon. What the hell was he doing?

Greg took the IV from her hands. 'Thanks, Doc.'

The noise of the plane deafened her. Confusion swirled with anger, making her speechless. As much as she wanted to hurl words at Huon, she couldn't argue with him in front of a patient.

The two men disappeared into the plane. Brendan closed the doors and a minute later the plane taxied down the airstrip.

Furious, Bronte watched the plane disappear into the blue sky. She wanted to scream at the plane. Scream at Huon. How could he have done that? He'd totally taken over without discussing anything with her. He'd literally stolen her patient.

He'd never done anything like that before. Sure, he'd hovered but had never completely taken over.

She did a quick calculation in her head. Huon would be back in six hours. When he stepped off the plane she'd be waiting for him. He had a hell of a lot of explaining to do.

Bronte stifled a yawn and looked at the clinic clock. Exhaustion clawed at her but she wasn't leaving until she'd spoken to Huon. She'd rehearsed ten times what she was going to say, hoping she could stay calm but really she was ready to throttle him.

She pictured her hands on his neck. But instead of life-threatening pressure she found the image more sensual, with her hands skimming across his skin up into the tendrils of hair that caressed his collar.

'Arrgh!' Her yell broke the silence of the clinic.

What was wrong with her? This man was her colleague. And right now he'd crossed an ethical boundary by accompanying *her* patient to Adelaide.

She needed to stay focussed. Not get sidelined by her attraction to him. An attraction she blamed totally on her pregnancy hormones.

But you can't just blame the pregnancy. She hated it when her rational self kicked in. Pregnant or not, Huon would have fascinated her, drawn her in like a moth to a flame.

He seemed to have no idea that his combination of rugged good looks, athleticism and caring approach sent her pulses pounding.

And it had to stay that way.

By the end of the night they would have established some working rules. Rules that would prevent this confusion from happening again. Rules that would help her keep her feelings for Huon in check. Rules that would reinforce that he was a fellow doctor, nothing else.

Hours later the buzz of the King Air sounded. She suppressed an urge to race outside and accost him. No, she would stay inside. Let him come to her.

She went into the clinic's kitchen and put the kettle on.

She plonked cutlery on the table, the sound of metal colliding with wood representative of her skittering thoughts.

She pulled out a platter of cold chicken and salad from the fridge, which Marg had sent over. Huon probably hadn't had a chance to eat.

The outside fly-wire door slammed shut, its thud reverberating down the corridor. Huon was back.

She hauled in a deep breath. *Stay calm, don't get angry, take it all slowly.*

'Bronte?' His deeply timbered voice called out her name.

'I'm in the kitchen.' *Stay calm.*

His firm and decisive footsteps sounded on the linoleum floor and he walked into the room. All six feet of him, looking handsome but exhausted.

Bronte squashed the flare of concern his fatigue always elicited. 'How's Tom?'

'Ventilated but stable, thank goodness.' He dropped into the chair and stretched his legs out in front of him. 'This looks great, thanks.' He picked up a drumstick and bit down into it.

'Marg sent it over.' She sat opposite him and spooned some potato salad, chicken and green salad onto her plate.

'Marg's a great cook and she's always wanted to feed me.' Huon grinned. 'Of course I don't object.' He loaded his plate with food. 'You're here late. I was worried there might have been another emergency, so I came in to check.'

She could feel her face tighten. 'Thought you'd come and take over another one of my patients, did you?'

'Sorry?' Confusion swam across his face. 'I came in

to see if everything was all right.' He looked straight into her face, his blue eyes darkening slightly. 'I'm worried you're working too hard. I came in to see if you needed a hand. You look tired and you know that only makes you extra-nauseous.'

The genuine concern in his voice disarmed her. She wanted to sink into that concern. But she couldn't. It wasn't personal concern, just professional.

Huon glanced around. 'Why are you here at seven o'clock on a Saturday night?'

'I'm here because I needed to talk to you about Tom.'

He poured them both a mug of tea. 'I would have rung you to let you know how he was.'

'I know. That's not the reason I'm here.'

He paused, his mug halfway to his mouth. He set it down and focussed his attention onto Bronte. 'OK,' He elongated the K.

Her words came out in a rush. 'I expected to be on that plane accompanying *my* patient to Adelaide.'

His brow creased for a moment in surprise. 'Oh. I guess as I've known Tom since he was born I just assumed I'd go with him.'

'If you apply that logic, I'll never do an evacuation with anyone except strangers to Muttawindi!' She blew out a breath, trying to keep calm, frustrated he thought this was no big deal. 'Today was your day off. You shouldn't have been here. I was the doctor in atten-dance. Why did you feel the need to check up on me?'

'Check up on you?' An expression of disbelief crossed his face. 'Hell, Bronte, you're a wonderful doctor. I totally trust you. I wouldn't have taken the day off if I didn't.'

'But that's the point. You didn't take the day off.'

'Of course I took the day off. I wasn't here this morning.'

'But you arrived at lunchtime! Why did you come in then?' She bit her lip to stop her voice rising.

'I just thought I'd call by and see how your radio clinic went.'

She crossed her arms. 'But I could have told you how it went at report meeting on Monday. You know, that day that follows the weekend, the weekend being those two days a lot of people don't come into work.'

He raised his brows. 'Sarcasm doesn't suit you. What do you really want to say?'

'How can I become an accepted part of this community if you keep turning up when you're rostered off and taking over? You know everyone in this town better than me. How can I get to know anyone if you won't share your patients?'

'Now you're being silly. Of course I share the patients.' He gave her a condescending smile. 'You can't rush this, Bronte. All you need is time and you'll get to know everyone.'

His expression and tone of voice flamed her frustration. 'No, I won't. Not if you won't let me. I don't think you're able to share this town with me. You can't stay away from the clinic, and you take over when you're here.' She rushed on, driven by his lack of understanding. 'In fact, I think the other doctors left because you wouldn't let them into the hallowed halls of Muttawindi.'

Huon's face tightened as anger and regret wove

across his face. He spoke quietly. 'Your predecessor wasn't a doctor.'

'What?' She must have misheard.

He ran his hand roughly through his hair. 'He wasn't a doctor. He had fake qualifications and posed as a doctor. I was exhausted when he arrived so I took a week off. In that time he managed to cause iatrogenic illnesses with medication and misdiagnose appendicitis. Lisa McQuilly's lucky to be alive.'

Oh my God. That was why the town was so wary of her. That was why Huon hovered over her.

He nodded. 'I blame myself.'

'But you weren't to know. Head Office would have hired him in good faith. You're not the first doctor to have something like this happen—it happened in Melbourne last year.'

'But I should have observed him. The town trusted me so they trusted him. I have to make it up to them. I owe them good medical care.'

Frustration whizzed through her. How did she counter irrational blame? 'You give them excellent medical care and so do I. That nightmare is over. You know I'm competent so now you can step back and relax.'

'It's not as simple as that. They depend on me.'

She heard her voice rise. 'And they can learn to depend on me. You need to let go. I need you to let go so I can get to know the town and have a chance of belonging. So the baby and I can be part of Muttawindi.' She had to make him understand. 'Hell, how can I compete with you, the local boy made good, the doctor who's second to God, their very own son, if you won't share the load and share the patients?'

Huon's face drained of colour. 'I'm not their son.'

She pushed her plate away. 'Oh, please, Huon. They idolise you. You're one of them, not an outsider like me.'

'I didn't arrive here until I was fourteen.'

Something in his voice made her look more closely at him. His eyes reflected an emotion she couldn't exactly pin down but part of her experienced a moment of pain.

'But I thought you were born here?'

'I was born in Adelaide.'

'Oh.' Surprise filled her. 'But your family originally came from here, right? They returned when you were a teenager?'

'No.' The word came out on a sigh.

Bronte noticed a slight shudder go through him. Something was going on here, something big. Whatever it was, Huon wasn't really offering it up. And she sensed that this story wouldn't be comfortable for him to tell.

But she also had a growing feeling it was important for her to hear it. 'Are you saying you were an outsider like me?' She tried to keep her voice light and not sound like an interrogator.

'I was. I arrived here an angry and belligerent teenager.'

She smiled. 'Most fourteen-year-olds don't want to move and leave their friends to come to a new place with their parents.' Bronte knew that feeling well.

'I didn't come with my parents.'

Questions raced across her mind but she stopped her tongue from asking them. Instead, she chose silence, hoping it would encourage him to tell his story.

Tension radiated from him. The usually rugged yet gentle planes of his face became sharp and pinched. 'My parents died when I was nine and I went into a group home.'

His words hit Bronte, winding her. Instinctively, she reached out her hand and covered his. 'Oh, God, I'm sorry.'

His blue eyes bored into her, hooded with pain. 'Yeah, it wasn't good.'

All her preconceived ideas about Huon crumbled. She'd been so certain he had a loving family, who featured largely in his life, especially when he'd been so adamant her child needed a family.

Huon's hand moved, his thumb caressing hers. A shiver of longing swept through her. 'How did you end up here in Muttawindi?'

He let go of her hand and sat back in his chair, silent for a moment. 'By a long, tortuous road.' His hurt was audible. 'I lived in the group home then with a few foster-families in Adelaide. By fourteen I was jack of the whole thing. I got in with a car-stealing gang and I landed up in front of a magistrate. He gave me a choice. Two years in a youth training centre or come out here.'

'And you chose here?' Bronte looked into his sky-blue eyes, now darkened with painful memories, and wished she could absorb some of his distress.

'I did. Best decision I've ever made. Ron and Claire took me in, made sure I was fed and clothed, made sure I went to school, and loved me.'

He gave a wry smile. 'Thank goodness they saw through my bravado, my tough-kid act. Between them and the town's people, like Marg, they showed me I could do a lot better in life than steal cars. They taught me I could do anything if I put my mind to it.'

Huon's words whizzed around Bronte's brain. He'd been dealt a lousy hand as a kid and yet he'd turned himself around completely. 'And Claire convinced you to do medicine?'

'She encouraged me. Muttawindi had never had a doctor. Claire was the remote area nurse in charge of the bush hospital. As I grew up, the town grew, too. With the gas fields opening, it seemed a logical choice to come back here as a doctor. Give back to the town that took me in. And Ellen agreed.'

'Ellen?' She tried to voice the word casually despite her desperation to know.

'My wife.' He sighed and swallowed hard. 'She died a couple of years ago.' His voice rasped out the words. 'The town had to rescue me a second time.'

His grief tore at her. No one deserved to lose their parents and their partner. 'I'm so very sorry.' Her words sounded hollow and useless against the pain in his voice. 'Life can be pretty unfair sometimes.'

An emotion she couldn't identify flickered behind his eyes. 'Yeah, some wonderful lives get cut short for no reason.'

Bronte watched his fingers trace the handle of his tea mug, trying to absorb his story. From street kid to husband, on to respected doctor and then widower. It was a hell of a roller-coaster journey in a short time. No wonder Huon had an incredibly strong connection to Muttawindi.

Suddenly everything fell into place. Huon thought he

owed the town everything. The town had cared for him during his darkest days and now he cared for the town. That's why he'd gone with Tom. It had nothing to do with not letting her be involved.

It was everything to do with Huon needing to be there for the town. His family.

He leaned in towards her. 'This town is a pretty amazing place.' He picked up her hand. 'I promise to let you get on with your job and I'll try not to step on your toes. You're needed here.'

His fingers on her hand set off mini-explosions inside her. She leaned towards him as if propelled by the force of his penetrating eyes. His scent of soap and dust enveloped her, and she breathed it in, searing it onto her memory.

He needed her. He wanted to kiss her.

Flames of longing danced in his eyes. The same fire that burned inside her. Did he feel the same attraction she did?

His head moved closer, his breath stroked her skin.

Stroked beneath her skin, stirring the simmering warmth which exploded into a raging heat that licked at every part of her.

Time stilled. Her heart pounded loudly against her ribs, the sound filling her ears. The air around her pressed in on her, hot, close, in anticipation of his kiss. A kiss which part of her wanted and part of her feared. An uncontrollable force edged her forward.

Huon tilted his head even closer, his hair brushing her face, his lips parting with a slight tremble.

Bronte closed her eyes, giving in to the inevitable moment, giving up the battle to fight the burning desire deep inside her. She longed for the soft pressure of his lips against hers. She ached to taste him and have him fill her throbbing need, a need that had grown from the moment she'd met him.

Abruptly Huon pulled back.

Her eyes flew open, seeking his. But his eyes now shuttered from any discernible emotion gave her no clues.

'Muttawindi really needs a doctor like you.' He dropped her hand.

Her skin chilled at the loss of his touch. Disappointment flooded her, dousing the heat.

Of course, the town. Huon saw everything in terms of Muttawindi. She understood that now. Huon needed her to stay because the town needed a second doctor. And he lived to care for the town. There was no room in his life for anyone else.

She'd misread all the signs again, just like with Damien. How had she been so stupid to let herself think Huon wanted her, even for a moment?

CHAPTER SIX

AN HOUR LATER, Huon pushed open his front door and dumped his keys on the hallstand. He headed down the long hall towards the kitchen, his footsteps echoing on the Baltic pine floorboards.

Pulling open the fridge, he reached for a stubby, twisted the cap, and raised it to his lips. The amber fluid, cold in his throat, felt good. It might be nine o'clock at night, but the heat hadn't lessened.

He slumped onto the couch, flicked on the TV and channel-surfed for a few moments. Satellite access, a myriad of channels and still nothing worth watching.

Damn. He tossed the remote onto the coffee-table. The silence of the house pressed in on him. Not even the cicadas were singing tonight. Loneliness surrounded him, squeezing him, making his chest tight.

His first official day off in a long time had come to an end. Except he'd taken Tom to Adelaide.

And opened the door to his past. Hell, he hated talking about it. Thankfully he didn't have to very often because everyone in town already knew his story.

And Bronte's initial look had been the same look of sadness and sympathy he always got which was why he avoided telling people. He didn't want to look back— his past belonged exactly there.

But after the sympathy in Bronte's huge grey eyes had faded, he'd glimpsed a tantalising fire of wanting.

Images of her long, slender neck flooded his mind. He longed to touch her cascading hair, plunge his face into it, and breathe in her intoxicating scent. And those round ruby lips…

His groin tightened at the thought. This woman was turning him inside out. He'd never reacted like this to a woman before.

Not even Ellen. He'd loved her dearly, but it had been a love that had evolved from adolescence. He'd met Ellen on his first day at uni, and she'd become his best mate. Marriage had been a natural extension of that loving friendship. A friendship that had turned into a deep, abiding love.

But Bronte had a magnetic effect that drew him in. Hell, he'd almost kissed her tonight. Her soft bottom lip had trembled, urging him to kiss her, to take what she was offering.

And he'd wanted to. God, how he wanted to.

But he couldn't. He wouldn't.

Bronte was pregnant, confused, and he wouldn't take advantage of her vulnerability. He didn't want to risk hurting her.

Hurting himself. He could never go through losing someone again. He'd managed to climb out of the black hole of grief when his parents had died, and then after Ellen. The thought of heading down there again terrified him.

No, he wouldn't put himself out there for that.

The town gave him care and friendship and that was all he needed.

All he had to do was think of Bronte as his colleague. His pregnant colleague. His job was to monitor the pregnancy and her workload. She tended to push herself to the limit and someone had to make sure she didn't overdo things.

Hell, he could do that.

So what if he wanted to caress and smooth out the worry lines on her forehead, if his fingers itched to tuck her hair behind her ear, and her laugh sent rivers of longing through him? He was a professional. He could lock down his feelings and be her colleague and her friend.

How hard could it be?

Huon pulled up in front of Bronte's house. The summer heat had given way to glorious autumn days. It was still warm but not stifling.

He'd taken to calling by, checking that everything was working well. Her old corrugated-iron cottage, Muttawindi's solution to termites, needed a few repairs. He enjoyed getting out his tools and seeing his handi-work improve things.

Huon picked up the picnic hamper Marg had packed for him. Bronte had mentioned she was going to paint this Sunday and, knowing Bronte, she wouldn't think to stop for lunch. She'd work until she dropped.

It was hard to believe how much energy she had

these days compared to the exhausted doctor who had arrived in town. But he didn't want her getting tired and sick. So he'd organised lunch. He'd drop it off and head straight out to Kintawalla and have a swim.

A quick visit. Nothing else. He wasn't staying. This was all part of antenatal care. *Yeah, right*. He was just making sure she was taking care of herself and the baby.

He walked around to the back door of her house, pulled open the fly-wire door and walked into the kitchen. 'Bronte? It's Huon.'

Footsteps sounded down the hall and Bronte appeared in the kitchen, holding a paintbrush. She'd piled her long hair on top of her head and held it back from her face with a scarf. A short, tight T-shirt hugged her breasts and over the top of it she wore a giant pair of overalls. They hung baggily from her shoulders, allowing for her growing pregnancy and some. Bare feet peeked out from under the rolled-up khaki fabric.

Her face glowed in a way only a pregnant woman's could. No longer gaunt from fatigue and nausea, but rounded and radiant, with a hint of justified pride.

And her patrician nose wore pale green paint.

Desire thundered through him. Bronte in old painting clothes was a far sexier woman than Bronte in her buttoned-up workclothes. He grabbed a steadying breath.

'Hi, Huon.' Surprise mixed with pleasure crossed her face. 'What brings you here?'

'I've brought you lunch.' Huon held up the basket.

'Oh, that's kind but you didn't have to. I could have rustled something up.'

'Really?' Huon walked over and opened her fridge.

'Would you have been having the mouldy cheese or the brown banana?'

'You're exaggerating. It isn't as dismal as that.'

Half indignant, half laughing, Bronte walked up behind him and peeked over his shoulder into the fridge.

He felt her closeness, her warmth radiating into him, her spicy scent encircling him, tempting his senses. His blood heated and his heart pounded. He wanted to move away, get some distance, but he was caught between Bronte and the fridge.

At least the fridge was cold.

'Look.' She pointed to the freezer. 'I have bread in there.'

'And not much to put on it.' He turned to face her, resisting the temptation to touch her, resisting the longing that pulled at him to wrap his arms around her and hold her close. That would be a disaster.

He sighed. 'You have to eat properly. You tell your patients that, and you need to take your own advice.'

For a moment she looked sheepish. 'You're right. Sorry, I got distracted by the nursery.' She waved her paintbrush in the direction of the hall. 'Come and look at it. I'm really pleased with how it's coming along and—'

'You need to stop for half an hour to eat.'

'Oh, all right. I can see I'm not going to win this round.' She laughed, put the paintbrush down and sat at the table, leaning back in the chair. She swung her feet up onto another chair and swung her arms out wide, her breasts straining against her T-shirt.

She gave him a wicked grin. 'I'm ready, so feed me.'

His breath stalled in his chest. This woman had no idea what her teasing did him. No idea of the effect she had on him. No idea of her sexuality.

And it had to stay that way.

Huon opened the basket, unloaded the contents onto plates and then picked the basket up again. 'Make sure you sit for half an hour.'

'Aren't you going to stay?' A brief streak of disappointment crossed her face. 'You can't just drop in lunch like meals-on-wheels and go. You have to eat too. Can't you spare twenty minutes?'

'No, I really need to—'

'Hey, if you can tell me I have to stop and take a break, I can tell you the same thing.' She pushed the second chair out with her foot and crossed her arms. 'Sit.'

In a reflex action to the tone of her voice Huon sat before he'd realised he had.

'Good.' Bronte raised her brows. 'See, it wasn't that hard, was it?'

Huon picked up a salad roll. 'I had no idea you were so bossy.'

'I learned it from you.' Bronte laughed and then poured a glass of water from the jug. 'You're really sweet, dropping around with lunch. I could get used to being looked after.' A wistful tone entered her voice.

Then she almost seemed to shake herself. She sat up straight and reached for the baguette filled with salad and tuna. 'I'm starving.' She bit down into the crunchy bread.

Her actions tore at him. He hated glimpsing the vulnerable Bronte. He didn't want to think about that, it was dangerous territory. It was much easier to think about the determined, focussed Bronte. The Bronte who worked hard, and who was totally centred on creating a lifestyle for herself and her baby. Mother and child united.

'Have you made your ultrasound appointment? You're eighteen weeks now so you need to get it done, plus you need to see John Phillips, the obstetrician at Broken Hill.'

She rolled her eyes. 'Yes, Doctor. I'll make the appointments on Monday if I have time.' She pursed her lips like an old-fashioned schoolmarm. 'But you're not on duty now so eat your lunch.'

He raised his brows at her avoidance tactic. 'I'll remind you on Monday.'

She poked her tongue out at him and grinned, looking like a cheeky sixteen-year-old.

The wildfire in his veins blazed again and he gulped down a glass of water. Time to change the topic. 'So I'm guessing you've got some paint on the wall and not just on you?'

She looked down at herself and laughed. 'I had a bit of fun with the roller. Oh, well, it doesn't matter, I never look good anyway, so maybe some paint might give me the allure I lack.'

'You look pretty good to me.' The words came out low and husky.

For a brief moment Bronte stilled. A flare of something sparked in her eyes then died. 'Yeah, right. I'm in the oldest, most ill-fitting clothes I own.'

'Yes, but you wear them with style. I actually like you more in this outfit than in your navy blue skirt and white high-neck blouse.' He spoke the words before his brain censored them.

She raised her brows. 'Well, then, you'll be pleased to hear the days of the skirt are over. I can't do up the zip.'

He'd committed himself to a dangerous road so he may as well continue. 'Great. Give it to the op-shop.'

'Huon!' Her eyes sparked in indignation.

'No, I'm serious. It's a skirt that should be worn by a fifty-year-old matron, not an adventurer like you.'

'I'm hardly an adventurer.'

'You've left behind the life you knew and come out here to start again. I'd call that adventurous.'

Bronte tilted her head and looked at him. 'I suppose when you put it like that, I could, at a stretch, be called adventurous. But it really doesn't matter what I wear, I never look any good.'

Huon remembered the first morning Bronte had spent in Muttawindi. He'd been struck by the fact that she wore clothes that were too old-fashioned for her, clothes that didn't flatter her. He'd realised she didn't seem to know she was beautiful. At the time he'd put it down to fatigue and nausea. No one felt gorgeous when they were about to throw up.

But now he wondered if there was more to it. 'You think you never look any good?' He tried to keep the disbelief out of his voice.

'I was once compared to a plucked chicken.'

'Well, you can forget what that creep told you, he only wanted to hurt you.' He tried to keep the anger that simmered inside him whenever he thought of Damien out of his voice.

'My mother and sister have always been keen to point out to me that I could look better.' She spoke lightly but with a trace of bitterness.

'Really?'

'Yes. Steph was the gorgeous girl. She loved the party clothes, the dress-ups, the accessories and make-up. And then there was me. Mum tried to dress me like Steph but I always felt wrong, overdressed, too tizzy.'

Images of Bronte's wardrobe flashed in front of him. Always sedate, always plain, almost puritanlike clothes.

'So you eventually rebelled against that and gave up all the tizz?'

Her face registered surprise. 'I suppose I did.' She fiddled with the edge of her plate. 'Look, clothes are a necessary evil to keep me warm or protect me from the sun. As long as they're functional, it really doesn't matter.'

'Ah, but that's where you're wrong. Mark Twain had it right when he said, "Clothes maketh the man."'

'Yeah, well, they don't maketh this woman.' A warning edge entered her voice.

Huon pushed on. 'Maybe you just haven't tried the right clothes.'

'What is this? When did you become a fashion guru?'

Huon laughed. 'I can't say that I'm one of those new "metrosexuals". But haven't you ever had a favourite outfit? One that when you wore it, you felt special?'

Bronte downed her water and refilled her glass, the only sound in the room the ice clinking against the tumbler.

Huon watched her tight expression as she dredged her memory against her better judgement.

'I had a pair of jeans once that I loved. Whenever I wore them as a kid I felt free and able to do anything. But Mum always insisted on dresses or skirts so the jeans went by the wayside.'

That was it. Bronte didn't relax in her clothes. That was the difference today. She was relaxed and at ease in her old overalls and her way-too-tight T-shirt. And her radiance shone through.

For some reason he needed her to recognise her own beauty. She needed to know she was gorgeous as well as a talented doctor. Maybe getting her to find her own style was the first step towards making her realise she was beautiful. 'None of your clothes are going to fit any more, are they?'

Bronte shook her head. 'No, and I dread having to buy a new wardrobe. I hate shopping for clothes.'

'Don't, then.'

'What?'

'Today you look sensational in old painting gear.'

Warring emotions played across her face. 'Huon, there is no way I can possibly look sensational.'

'Bronte, believe me, you look great and you're comfy, right?'

'Yes, but I can't wear these clothes to work!'

'Maybe not the T-shirt.' He gave her a grin. 'Although it might be the way to get old Jack onside.'

He laughed at her blush.

'If you feel comfortable, that's half the battle. Tune in to the adventurer in you. An adventurer needs new clothes. You loved the freedom those jeans offered you, so go for clothes that give you the same feeling.'

'But it's too hot for jeans.' Her voice sounded strained, filled with a mixture of old hurt and apprehension.

'Choose shorts, then. Think outside the square. Instead of replacing your wardrobe with maternity-type clones, go for the adventurer-outback look. You might just surprise yourself.'

Bronte pushed her now empty plate away in an almost defiant action. 'Huon, I think you need to stick to medicine—you're good at that. But fashion advice, I don't think so.'

He looked at her sceptical face and sighed. How did you convince someone they were beautiful when they couldn't see it? She deserved to know that; she deserved to see herself as she really was. Brave and beautiful.

He had no idea how he was going to open her eyes to her own beauty but he'd give it a go. After all, that's what colleagues did—they looked out for each other, right?

Bronte waved Huon goodbye and wandered back to her painting. She dipped the brush into the tin, ran the bristles against the edge to drain the excess paint and started to cut in around the door.

Huon had taken to dropping in. He usually arrived to fix something or to give her something. It had started a few weeks ago with her blood-test results. Today it had been lunch. Whatever it was, he never stayed long. He'd only stayed today because she'd bulldozed him into it.

Since the night she'd challenged him on not being able to share the patients, the night he'd opened up about his past, the night she'd so stupidly thought he would kiss her, his behaviour had lurched between being her colleague and doctor, and being a friend.

It was like he couldn't make up his mind. She had the feeling he regretted opening up to her. But if he did want to keep things strictly professional and only work-related contact, why was he dropping in to fix her hot-water service, fix the drooping curtain rail or remind her about appointments she should make?

It was a friendship that was tearing her apart.

She wanted so much more.

But he was still grieving for his wife.

You look pretty good to me. Huon's low, husky voice kept replaying in her mind. Why would he have said that? Did friends say stuff like that? No one had ever really told her she looked good, except for Damien's lies, which didn't count. Compliments about her appearance had been so few and far between she couldn't really remember hearing any. As a child she had constantly been compared to Steph, and found to be sadly lacking.

And for Huon to give her a compliment when she was covered in paint, she couldn't work it out. Bronte placed her paintbrush down on the drop sheet and walked over to the cheval mirror. Her image looked back at her. Plain and paint-splattered.

She knew Huon hadn't been teasing her, so why would he have said what he had? She looked again. Her face was more round now, giving her a softer look. Her hair had grown since she'd arrived in Muttawindi and curled gently around her face. Her breasts had defi-nitely grown. For the first time ever, she had some.

She ran her hand over her stomach and cupped the

small bulge that had popped out in the last few weeks. 'Hey, baby, you're making some changes. I wouldn't say I'm pretty, but maybe I'm not quite as plain.'

Suddenly she thought of the catalogue that Claire had given her last week. At the time she'd shoved it in her bag, not really wanting to look at it.

Bronte rummaged through the pile of reading on her desk and found it. She turned the pages and looked at the maternity clothing, wondering if Huon's fashion advice had any merit. Towards the back of the catalogue she found a pair of maternity cargo shorts and a contrasting sleeveless white shirt, decorated with large, bold, indigo flowers.

She could see herself wearing something like that.

Her mother and Stephanie's fashion instructions boomed in her head. She tossed the catalogue aside. She wasn't one to give in to flights of fancy. The paint fumes must have got to Huon, making him say things he didn't mean.

She looked like a pregnant woman. Nothing more, nothing less. Nothing to write home about. She was reading more into a silly conversation than she should.

Bronte picked up her paintbrush and then turned up the CD really loud, hoping to blast all the voices out her head, especially Huon's.

But the catalogue kept drawing her attention.

Maybe she could order one thing, just to try it out?

She'd think about it tomorrow.

Bronte struggled to tie up the X-ray gown and eventually pulled a second one on to hide the split back. She didn't fancy her bottom being on public display when she walked into the ultrasound room.

Dignity got parked at the door in hospitals, and Broken Hill Base was no different. She'd come in to Broken Hill for her twenty-two-week ultrasound, sharing the plane with Huon who had a meeting with the hospital's chief medical officer.

Actually, Huon had harangued her into coming. He'd pointed out in no uncertain terms that the ultrasound should have been at eighteen weeks. He'd gone ahead and made the appointment for her and booked her on the flight. She hadn't been able to put it off any longer.

Going to an ultrasound on her own wasn't something she was putting her hand up for. There was something about the routine ultrasound that screamed 'happy expectant couples'. It was one of those pregnancy things you did with the father of your baby.

But Huon was right—she couldn't avoid it any longer, no matter how much she might wish her situation were different. So here she was, waiting. Alone. Butterflies batted in her stomach. It seemed silly to be nervous but she was about to meet her baby 'on screen'.

'Dr Hawkins.' The young female radiographer called her name.

Clutching her gown close to her, she walked into the room and clambered up onto the examination table.

'Would you like me to video the ultrasound so you can take it home to your partner?' She bustled about, warming the gel and checking the transducer.

Bronte swallowed against the lump in her throat that rose every time she thought about the fact she was doing this pregnancy and parenthood gig all on her own. 'A photo will be just fine, thanks.'

The lights dimmed, the warm gel hit her belly and the transducer pressed down on her skin. The machine blipped and pinged and suddenly a white shape appeared on a black background. Floating on its back like a film star in a luxury swimming pool was her baby, nonchalantly sucking its thumb.

She gasped as a tidal wave of emotion swept through her. Joy, happiness and apprehension, all wrapped up together, exploded inside her. Tears pricked the backs of her eyes as wonder took over.

She tried to listen attentively to the radiographer as she called out the crown-rump length and the biparietal circumference measurements of the baby. Tried to be a doctor. But her gaze was riveted to the picture on the screen.

My baby.

The door opened and a shaft of light dazzled her, silhouetting the tall figure in a doctor's coat. The door closed behind him.

'I thought you might like some company.' Huon's deep voice warmed her as he sat down on the swivel stool next to her.

Gratitude filled her, mixed fleetingly with something she couldn't name. She blinked back tears. He'd known what a momentous occasion this was and he hadn't wanted her to be alone. 'Thanks.'

'Pretty cute kid.' He grinned at her, a grin full of pure delight as his gaze took in the somersaulting foetus.

He'd come to the ultrasound. 'Takes after me.' The

quip hid the roller-coaster of feelings surging inside her. His grin always undid her, but combined with his thoughtfulness and caring she didn't know if she wanted to laugh, cry or sing.

'You're just in time to hear the baby's heartbeat, Doctor.' The radiographer positioned the transducer and suddenly the room filled with the sound of racing horses' hooves.

New life.

'One hundred and twenty-six beats per minute.' The radiographer's voice sounded over the boom of the heartbeat.

'Perfect.' Huon breathed out the word.

He squeezed Bronte's hand, his heat racing through her veins. Words jumbled in her brain and jammed in her throat. He was here, sharing this moment. Feeling the same awe and wonder.

Her heart beat faster. He wanted to be here with her. With her and the baby. She held his hand tighter.

Suddenly, Huon dropped her hand and stood up, moving closer to the screen. 'Is the placenta high on the uterine wall?' His tone was brisk and businesslike as he faced the radiographer, his back to Bronte.

'No sign of placenta praevia. No sign of anything untoward. The baby looks great and everything lines up with a twenty-two-week gestation.' The radiographer indicated all the measurements on the side of the screen.

'Excellent. Make sure I get a copy of that report.'

He looked at his watch. 'Bronte, I'll see you back at Reception. I just have to catch up with the orthopaedic registrar about a hip replacement.'

He gave a quick wave, the door swung open and slammed shut. Her doctor had left the building.

Her doctor.

It was a surreal moment. For one brief minute, when Huon had squeezed her hand, her fantasy of sharing her pregnancy with him had seemed real.

Now it was vapour.

Disappointment crept through her, oozing into deep crevices, taking hold.

He'd been doing his job. Just like he always did his job. He always treated his patients as people, never as numbers. He'd been extending that same care and courtesy to her because she was his patient.

And she knew that. Why was she lapsing into a fantasy world? Why did she let herself think she was any more special than any other of his patients?

She wasn't. But she wished so much that she was.

The letter in Huon's hand weighed less than twenty grams but it sat heavy against his palm. He'd collected the mail from Head Office while Bronte had been seeing the obstetrician.

Now she sat opposite him in the plane, her eyes closed, her face relaxed and at peace, enjoying a rare moment of not having to do anything or be anywhere. He could sit and watch her for the entire journey.

Did he want to break that moment and let reality intrude? The image of her radiant face shining with the miracle of seeing her baby *in utero* had been on constant replay in his mind for the last two hours.

What had he been thinking when he'd gone into the

ultrasound room? He'd been monitoring her pregnancy for three months and he'd thought he could be the doctor and stay detached. But seeing Bronte's baby doing backstroke across the screen had ripped open feelings he'd put aside a long time ago. He and Ellen had talked about children but that hope was lost to him now.

The baby and Bronte belonged together as a unit. She was still sorting her life out, and had her own issues to grapple with. She wasn't emotionally ready for a relationship.

And he sure as hell wasn't.

He turned the letter through his fingers. It was addressed to Bronte. The return address read, 'Damien Cartwright, Melbourne.' Bronte must have written to him like she'd said she would.

He shouldn't care what was in the letter. It was nothing to do with him. But what if the father of the baby wanted a role in Bronte's life? He didn't want to think about that.

Bronte was a woman with a lot of guts and determination. She'd cope with whatever Damien had written. But he had an overwhelming urge to want to protect her. Keep her in Muttawindi. Keep her safe from any more hurt.

But he couldn't.

'Did the mail come?' Bronte stretched and leaned forward, her eyes sparkling in anticipation. 'I'm expecting a package.'

'No, packages, just this letter.'

She took it from his outstretched hand, turned it over and stilled. Her eyes sought his. 'It's from Damien.'

'I know.'

He'd expected apprehension in her eyes. But he saw surprise quickly followed by resignation. 'You'll want to open it when you're alone.'

She shook her head. 'You know the whole story so I'd rather deal with it now.' With a slight tremble in her hand she peeled open the envelope.

He watched her closely, looking for a hint of reaction, fearing the contents would change the course she had chosen for her life. Fearing they would affect him.

She dropped the letter in her lap and smiled up at him. 'He doesn't want any contact.'

'He's not marching into town?' He tried to sound flippant, to hide his relief that Damien Cartwright wanted no part in Bronte's life.

'He's given me the address of his lawyer for the future "should the child wish to make contact when he is older".' She shoved the letter back into the envelope. 'Thank goodness that's over. I doubted he'd want any involvement but knowing for certain is a huge relief.'

Her grey eyes sparkled as she looked at him and smiled. The wariness and worry that had tagged her since her arrival in Muttawindi had fallen away, replaced by expectation and hope. 'Now I can really start to live here, and in a month or so when the house is painted I'll tell Mum and Dad about the baby.'

It was as if she'd had an emotional make-over.

Passion and zeal shone through, making his own carefully constructed life look grey and listless.

But he'd spent two years crafting his life. It was what he wanted, what he needed.

Wasn't it?

CHAPTER SEVEN

IT HAD BEEN a busy few weeks and today's full day clinic was no exception. The late afternoon sun bore down hot and strong under the veranda at Marmambool Station. Bronte could feel the sweat trickling down her back. So much for an outback winter. The seasons seemed to have forgotten to move along.

The baby kicked her from under her new sleeveless shirt. After her initial hesitation she'd found she really enjoyed shopping by catalogue. 'Yeah, I know, it's been a long day. Almost home time.' She rubbed her belly where the foot had pummelled her. She longed to collapse on the couch at home. Although only at the beginning of her third trimester, she was starting to tire more easily.

She glanced over at Huon and was struck by the sight of his blond hair, in stark contrast to the tight black curls of the Aboriginal preschooler who sat on his lap. The little girl had his stethoscope in her ears and had stuck the end of it under Huon's shirt. He was pretending to be sad while she patted him on the arm.

She swallowed hard. The image of Huon and the

child lanced her deeply. Her child would have no father. And no man would want to take on another man's child. The baby kicked again. Bronte blinked rapidly. She was *not* going to cry at work.

Right now just about anything set her off. Television commercials for overseas phone calls, fathers kissing babies' feet on nappy promotions, and a blond and blue-eyed doctor who had no idea the effect he had on her.

Wherever she went, she had people singing the praises of Huon. And rightly so. He was a wonderful, caring doctor. But, combined with her working with him so closely most days, it gave her precious little time to recover and armour up her heart for the next day. She needed the privacy of her own home to do that.

Her feelings for Huon had only grown and intensified. She longed for the glimpses of the Huon who had held her hand at the ultrasound, who had been awed by the sight of the baby. But he was back to being polite but distant.

'Are you all right, Bronte?' Claire's concerned voice broke into her thoughts. Claire had been mothering her ever since the pregnancy had shown itself.

She pulled her face into what she hoped was a smile. 'Fine, just a bit tired.'

But Claire had followed her line of vision. 'He'd make a great father.' She looked closely at Bronte. 'He and Ellen had planned to have children but, like all their plans, they got cut short.'

Bronte grabbed the opportunity she'd waited weeks for. 'What was Ellen like?'

'She was a warm and generous woman who loved the

outdoors.' Claire sighed. 'She worked as an engineer out on the gas fields, doing a job she loved, but a gas leak and explosion took her from us.' Claire gave Bronte a knowing look. 'I don't suppose he's told you anything about her?'

'No…but I guess he finds it hard to talk about her.'

'It's time he was past grieving.'

The matter-of-fact tone in Claire's voice shocked her. 'I don't think there is a time limit on grief, is there?'

'I think there has to be. Ellen wouldn't have wanted him to live alone. As his foster-mother, it's hard watching him put his life on pause. It's time he pressed the play button and moved on.'

'I suppose he'll move on when he's ready.'

Claire's eyes bored into Bronte's face. 'I think he's ready, he just doesn't know it. He needs someone to show him he's ready.'

Claire's scrutiny had her cringing inside. Were her feelings for Huon so obvious?

Carving out a life in Muttawindi was hard enough, without the residents seeing her heart bleeding on her sleeve. Without them knowing that the plain doctor who had got herself knocked up had the hots for their doctor. Without them knowing that Huon never looked at her twice, no matter how much she wanted him to.

She wanted to run and hide in a dark place and be alone. But she couldn't do that. She had to squelch the hopeful look in Claire's eyes. She had to put this rumour or thought process or whatever it was to bed right now.

She had to lie through her teeth.

'Well, I wish him well. He obviously enjoyed being

married and I hope he finds someone who will love him.' Bronte avoided looking at Claire and turned to walk away.

'Bronte!' The command in Huon's voice carried down the veranda, making her turn sharply. He only used a tone like that when he was worried. She knew the moment she heard his voice that going home had just got delayed.

Craig Bennett, the young roustabout she had examined earlier in the day, stood next to Huon, his face streaked with fear. Huon had his hand on the youth's shoulder.

'Bring the resus kit, we've got a man down.'

She nodded, grabbed her medical boxes and ran down the veranda steps towards the two men. 'What's happened?'

Craig's voice wobbled. 'We were loading cattle onto the truck and Reg got jammed between the truck and the rail. Cattle stood on him.' His face paled to alabaster white. 'Doc, his bone's sticking out of his leg.' Craig twitched and then dropped in a dead faint.

'Claire!' Bronte's and Huon's voices merged.

Claire rushed over. 'I'll look after him. You two go and attend to Reg and I'll radio Broken Hill.'

Bronte stowed the medical kits in the ute and jumped into the cabin. The moment her bottom touched the seat Huon gunned the engine. She raised her brows as a plume of dust enveloped them

He gave her a grin. 'Sorry. The only excuse I get to drive fast is in an emergency.' He slowed down a fraction in deference to the gravel road as he drove towards the mustering area.

'Over there.' Bronte pointed to the cattle yard and the circle of men who had their hats in their hands.

Bronte ran over to the group, her medical case jolting her knees and the baby doing somersaults. She was worried about what she would find. On the short journey she'd been thinking through the worst case scenario. What if the cattle had trampled more than his leg?

A man who looked to be in his fifties lay on the ground, his face contorted with pain. Bronte dropped to her knees.

'Reg, I'm Bronte Hawkins. I'm a doctor.' She put her fingers to his carotid pulse, which pumped thinly under her fingers. She'd expected a thready pulse so no surprise there. The shocked man was bleeding but was it only into his leg?

'Reg, I know this sounds a dumb question, but where does it hurt?'

'Me leg doesn't tickle, Doc.' He gave her a look of incredulity.

'Anywhere else?' She whipped up his shirt and examined his chest, noting his breathing wasn't laboured. She gently palpated his abdomen, feeling his liver and spleen. 'Did you get trampled anywhere else?'

'Nah, Craig managed to pull me out. I'll have to thank him for that.'

'How is he?' Huon put down a larger medical kit next to the resuscitation gear Bronte had carried. 'Any abdominal injuries?'

'Looks like he was really lucky that way. No sign of flail chest, no abdominal tenderness.'

Huon knelt down next to her, his shirtsleeve brushing

her arm in an unconscious caress. 'Do you want to do the IV or the leg?'

She turned to her patient. 'Any preferences, Reg?' She was slowly undoing the damage of 'Dr Disaster' by giving people choices.

'Me leg's bloody sore. I reckon a woman's touch wouldn't go astray there.'

Bronte smiled and resisted the temptation to hug the injured man.

Huon gave a mock look of indignation. 'Hey, I can be gentle.'

'Doc, I've still got the bruises from the last examination you gave me.' The stockman's brave front faded as a spasm of pain hit him.

Huon put his hand on Reg's arm in a reassuring gesture. 'Lie still and a bit less cheek. Let us do the work.'

Bronte reached into the medical kit and grabbed the scissors. 'Sorry, Reg, but I'm going to have to cut your moleskins so I can treat your leg.'

'It's the least of me worries, Doc.'

The cut fabric folded back to expose part of his femur protruding from a jagged gash. Bronte's stomach plummeted. She'd hoped the injury would be to the tibia. This sort of injury was both life and leg threatening.

She looked at her watch. Time was vital. He needed to be in Theatre within three hours or he had a high risk of losing his leg.

'BP ninety on sixty-five.' The worry in Huon's voice matched her own.

They needed to stop the bleeding and bring up Reg's

blood pressure. 'As soon as I've doused this wound with Betadine, I'll put on a pressure bandage. Do you have Haemaccel?'

Huon nodded. 'I'm putting in two lines. One of Hartmann's, and one of Haemaccel. It's his best option until he can have a blood transfusion.'

She poured the antiseptic wash over the wound, the brown liquid spilling down Reg's leg into the red soil. Having a cattle hoof inside your leg wasn't going to make it a clean wound. It would be debrided in Theatre but meanwhile she could help minimise the damage of bacteria going wild.

Little Tom Tigani flashed through her mind. 'When did you last have a tetanus shot, Reg?'

'Last year, when I was fencing over at Blaketon.'

'Great.' One thing ticked off the list. But the worry about gangrene was ever present. He needed a bolus dose of penicillin.

'Are you allergic to penicillin?' Huon's voice mirrored her thoughts. This happened all the time. In emergencies their minds worked in unison. It was a shame some of that *simpatico* couldn't be translated to other parts of her life.

'No, Doc, not allergic to anything I know of.'

Bronte applied a gauze dressing and the pressure bandage to the wound. Then she pressed her fingers into Reg's foot, trying to find a pedal pulse. Fractures like this could cut off the blood supply to the lower leg. She felt around his ankle, gently probing. Nothing.

She felt again, taking her time, being thorough. Still nothing.

She swore silently. This wasn't good for Reg. 'Can you feel my hands on your foot?'

'Sort of. It's a kinda fuzzy feeling.' His stoic look wavered for a moment. 'Me leg's gunna be all right, isn't it?'

Bronte didn't want to lie to him. She looked towards Huon in the slight hope she'd been overreacting. But deep furrows of concern brought his brows together in an uncharacteristic way. When Huon looked like that, things were bad.

This was no ordinary, straightforward fracture. Reg had no blood supply to his leg and now it looked like nerve damage, too. 'It's a nasty break, Reg. We're doing everything we can to save your leg.'

He gasped in shock and pain. 'Do you mean I might lose it?'

'Not if we can help it. But you're going to need surgery, a rod inserted into your leg, and traction. You'll be out of action for a long time.'

She tried to put some spin on the situation. 'Luckily, Gerald Robertson, the orthopaedic surgeon from Sydney, is in Broken Hill for a week, doing hip replacements. So we have an expert right here, and you won't have to go to Adelaide.' Considering the time factor, that could mean the difference between saving and losing the leg.

Reg groaned and closed his eyes for a moment.

He needed pain relief. 'Do you take any prescription medication?'

Reg shook his head.

'Do you have asthma or other lung problems, liver problems?'

'No, Doc, I'm generally pretty fit and well.'

She gave him a wan smile. 'Well, that's a plus at least. Right now we need to improve the blood supply up to your leg. I'm going to put a Donway splint on it to get the bone aligned. But before I do that I'll give you a morphine injection for pain relief. It will make you feel a bit sleepy.'

Huon finished taping the IV against Reg's arm and then called one of the station hands over. 'Reece, can you hold this bag of fluid nice and high for me?'

The man stepped forward, eager to help. 'Sure, Doc, no worries.'

Bronte drew up the morphine. 'Huon, ten milligrams of morphine.' She tapped the air bubbles out of the syringe.

She saw Huon's nod of acknowledgement. Dangerous drugs had to be accounted for at all times. She plunged the needle quickly and deeply into Reg's thigh.

Huon gently touched her arm. 'Would you like a hand with the splint?'

His eyes looked straight into her soul. She knew he could see how worried she was about Reg's leg. If the splint couldn't restore the blood supply, Reg faced amputation. Huon, in his usual way of caring for everyone, had made sure he was available to help her if she wanted it.

And she did want his help. Trauma medicine was all about teamwork. 'Yes, please.' She prepared the splint by adjusting the length to match Reg's leg length.

'Ready when you are.' Huon gave her a reassuring smile and a bolt of longing streaked through her. To him it was just a smile. To her it represented everything she wanted and knew she couldn't have.

She focussed on the splint application. 'I'll strap the ankle, you do the upper thigh.' She turned to Reg. 'The great thing about this splint is that we don't have to lift your leg, but it might hurt as I position your foot.'

'Just do what you have to do, Doc.' He spoke the words bravely, trying to mask his fear.

She gently placed his foot against the backboard of the splint and crossed the webbing around his foot, keeping it flexed upward.

The stockman's face blanched and he gripped Reece's ankle.

'Almost there, Reg. Huon, are your straps in position?'

'Yes, you can inflate the pump now.'

She activated the pump. With the pneumatic traction in place, she checked for pulses again. She prayed the splint would have aligned the bone and removed the pressure from the arteries.

Her fingers detected a faint pulse. Relief rushed through her and she wanted to high five Huon. 'Pulses present, thready but present.'

His grin said it all. 'Great! We're ready to roll. Where's Brendan?'

'Right behind you, Huon.' The pilot's baritone voice startled Bronte.

She laughed in surprise. 'That was perfect timing. Right, Reg, we're going to lift you up onto the stretcher. With the splint on and the morphine, you shouldn't feel too much discomfort.'

Brendan and Huon moved forward to lift Reg. Bronte didn't protest. She'd accepted that pregnancy and heavy lifting didn't go together.

Bronte looked at her watch. 'Brendan, can we be in Broken Hill within two hours?'

'Weather's clear. We should make it.'

That should mean the leg could be saved. But with a crush injury like that, she couldn't rule out a fat embolism. The next seventy-two hours would be crucial.

'Let's get going, then.'

Four hours later Bronte was back in Muttawindi. Brendan had made the trip in one hour, forty-five minutes, giving the orthopaedic surgeon some room to manoeuvre in Theatre and hopefully save Reg's leg.

She'd ring the hospital in a few hours. But right now exhaustion dragged at her, and all she wanted to do was go home. She picked up her bag to walk home, planning to collapse onto her couch the moment she stepped through the door. And close the door firmly on another emotionally exhausting day, working with a man who had no idea she was a woman as well as a colleague.

She had eight desperately needed Huon-free hours to get ready for another day.

Well, eight hours when he was physically not in her space. She knew her dreams would be filled with images of his dimples, unruly cowlick and a smile that melted her every time she experienced its rays. And recently a baby had entered the dreams, snuggled in Huon's strong, tanned arms.

She rubbed her temples, which throbbed at the thought.

'You need an early night.' Huon walked towards her, his car keys in his hand.

He had no idea that he was the cause of her restless

nights. Him and the baby, who usually took up gymnastics at three a.m.

His eyes zeroed in on her walking shoes. 'Come on, I'll drive you home.'

'Thanks, Huon, but the walk will be good.'

'It's dark outside and you're dead on your feet. I'm driving you home.'

She didn't have the energy to argue. She could handle another five minutes with Huon. After all, what was five minutes after a full day?

He opened the car door for her and then walked around to the driver's side. 'So, did you get Graeme Elliot over to look at that wiring in the kitchen I was worried about?'

A stab of guilt pierced her. Huon had been doing a pretty good impression of Mr Fixit, helping out with handyman-type things. He'd reminded her once already about the electrician. 'It's on my to do list. I got sidetracked with organising the nursery.'

Concern creased his forehead. 'I'll ring him if you like.'

Part of her wanted to say yes, but she had to stand on her own two feet. She was big girl and soon to be a mother. And Huon's brand of task-oriented friendship was increasingly hard to deal with when she wanted so much more. 'That's kind of you, but I'll do it tomorrow.'

She rested her head on the headrest and closed her eyes, mostly because she knew Huon wouldn't press her with her eyes shut. She felt the car turn twice and knew she was almost home. Almost home free, Huon free.

Coloured lights flashed against her eyelids as the four-wheel-drive stopped abruptly. Bronte opened her eyes.

'What's happened?' A fire engine blocked the short street.

'Don't know, but we need to find out. I'll grab my bag in case we need it.' He hopped out of the car.

She opened her door and the acrid smell of burning wood and melting plastic stung her nostrils. She jogged to join Huon.

They walked quickly around the front of the fire engine. A wall of heat forced them back.

Bronte gasped and gripped Huon's arm. Flames leapt out of her beloved 'tinny' house. Exploding glass shattered into the night and the corrugated-iron walls that resisted the termites so well buckled in the extreme heat.

An almighty roar rent the air as the crackling sound of the fire combined with a deafening crash and the roof caved in.

'Oh, my God!' She couldn't bear to look.

She felt Huon's arm around her as she buried her face in his shoulder. Great sobs racked her chest.

She had no house and no possessions. Desolation speared her heart. Now she and the baby were truly alone.

Huon looked on in horror as Bronte's house exploded in front of his eyes. The volunteer firefighters had no hope against such an inferno.

Bronte slumped against him. He had to get her away, get her somewhere safe. 'Come on, Bronte, I'll take you home.'

She looked at him, her eyes wide and uncomprehending, her feet not moving.

In a reflex action he picked her up, cradling her in

his arms, and carried her to the car. Her warmth flooded him, his arms tingling where they touched curves and hollows as he held her tightly against him.

He gently put her in the passenger seat, fastened her seat belt and then started the car. Bronte remained silent, staring straight ahead.

He kept glancing at her, worry eating into him as he drove the short distance to his house, holding her hand between gear changes.

She started to shake. Shock settled in.

'We're here.'

She sat unable to move yet her body shook on its own accord.

He lifted her out of the car and took her inside, laying her on the couch. He ran into his bedroom, whipped the cotton blanket off his bed and headed back to the lounge room.

'Here.' He tucked the blanket around her, wrapping it around her shoulders. 'I just want to check you and the baby, OK?'

She nodded silently.

He took her blood pressure. 'That's fine, but I want to listen to the foetal heart.'

Again the silent nod, followed by an almost automatic action of pulling up her blouse. The sleeveless blouse with bold blue flowers on it that he'd been admiring all day.

He did a quick abdominal examination to find the lie of the baby and, using the Pinard, he lent his ear to the trumpet stethoscope. He heard the rapid heartbeat, like horses' hooves racing against turf.

Thank God.

Relief moved through him but was quickly overtaken by something else. The feelings that had stirred when he'd been at the ultrasound grew. The memory of wanting to be a father, a longing to create a family.

He sat up and stowed the Pinard away, hoping to stow the feelings away as well. They didn't belong in his new life. 'You and the baby are fine. All you need is a strong, hot cup of tea with a truckload of sugar.'

Still she shook, eyes bleak with despair seeking his. 'The baby and I have nothing.'

Her desolation lashed him. This beautiful, brave woman was falling apart in front of him. He couldn't let her do that.

He sat down next to her and picked up her hand, which was cool to his touch. He covered it with his other hand. 'The important thing is that you weren't in the house tonight when the fire started.'

'I should have called the electrician. You kept reminding me, I—'

'Shh, it might not have been the wiring. It happened and it's over. You're safe, the baby's safe. We can replace the house and the possessions.'

'I…I don't even have any clothes.' The reality of the situation was slowly sinking in.

'It's a shame all of those great new clothes went up in flames. Still, now you have the perfect excuse for a totally new wardrobe.' He gave her a grin.

She looked up at him through thick brown lashes. 'I just didn't think I would be starting motherhood in a small room in a country pub.'

His world tilted. 'You can't stay at the pub.' The words shot out before he had a chance to think.

He couldn't let her live in the pub. Not when the station workers drove into town and whooped it up until the early hours of Sunday morning.

He ran his hands through his hair. He didn't want to offer his house but he had no choice. Bronte would have to live with him. Sweat broke out on his forehead. Sharing a house with her scared the hell out of him. Seeing her every day at work was hard enough, but now it would be out of hours as well.

'You can stay here.' His chest tightened. Her scent would be in the bathroom. She'd be sleeping in the spare bedroom next to his and eating breakfast with him in the mornings.

He'd just lost his buffer zone.

'Are you sure about this, Huon?' Her eyes sought his.

Hell, no. He was only sure it was a bad idea, but it was the only option open to him. He reached out and gave her a reassuring pat, forcing his voice to be light. 'Hey, what are friends for?'

Suddenly she was reaching for him, her arms going around his neck, her fingers lacing against his skin, her breasts pressing against his chest.

Her perfume, which reminded him of hot, tropical nights, sent a white bolt of heat through him. He buried his face in her hair and breathed deeply.

Her fingers unlaced and trailed along his jaw, driving showers of sensation into every part of him. 'Thank you.'

Two words whispered in a husky voice drove every rational thought from his mind.

She leaned forward, her ruby lips capturing his in a gentle but searing caress.

She tasted of salt and tears, heat and spice. Her lips opened slightly and he extended the kiss, delving deeper, exploring the world she offered to him.

She sighed against his mouth and fire exploded inside him. He pulled her closer, feeling all of her against him, wanting to feel her skin against his, wanting her heat to mix with his.

The baby kicked him.

Sanity returned.

He needed distance.

He had to get off this couch, out of this room. He stood up abruptly. 'Sorry, you're exhausted and you need to sleep. I'll get your room organised.'

Sleep. That was the last thing Bronte could think about. She watched him hurriedly leave the room. She struggled to get her breathing under control. Huon's kiss had been like sweet nectar flowing in her veins.

He'd tasted of sunshine and fresh air. She'd longed for his kiss, and it had exceeded her fantasies. His mouth, hot and welcoming, had probed her own, unlocking quivering waves of sensations she hadn't known she could experience.

And then he'd abruptly pulled away.

The look of horror on his face stayed with her, etched on her mind. Sympathy had for a moment spiralled out of control. And he'd quickly realised his mistake. She was his colleague, a friend perhaps, but nothing more.

Reality crushed her. She'd kissed him. It had all come

from her. Huon didn't desire her. He was still grieving for his wife.

In her heart she'd always known it. Now she had the evidence. He'd pulled away so fast it had been as if she'd been toxic.

She breathed in hard and deep to steady herself. She had a baby to provide for. She could do this. So her house had burnt down and she didn't even have a change of undies. But she had a job. She could buy new undies.

A hysterical laugh bubbled up inside her but she squashed it. She couldn't fall apart now. The thread of determination inside her tightened.

She'd been thrown a curve ball but she wouldn't let it faze her. Muttawindi kept throwing her challenges. She could rise to them. But sharing a house with Huon might be the hardest challenge she'd ever had.

CHAPTER EIGHT

Huon concentrated on making breakfast. *Eggs, bacon, tea, Vegemite, butter*. He ran the ingredients through his head as he walked into the pantry. He knew reciting lists in his head wasn't a good sign. But any distraction techniques to keep his mind off the curvy, chestnut-haired woman sleeping two rooms away were worth trying.

Last night's kiss had been playing in his mind half the night. He could still feel the touch of her skin against his and the heat of her mouth as he'd drunk in her taste.

He needed to forget all the desires that kiss had sparked. He didn't want to crave that sort of intimacy. It wasn't safe. And yet last night, when sleep had finally claimed him, it had come from knowing she and the baby were safe and sheltered in his house.

But he wasn't thinking about that. No, he was focussing on the facts. Yesterday he had lived alone. Today he had a housemate. A very temporary housemate, hopefully. After breakfast he'd ring Head Office, get the details of the insurance company and get the ball rolling.

All plans needed to lead to Bronte being moved into her new place before the baby was born. She needed her own space to lead the life she so desperately wanted for her and her baby.

And the idea of a mother and child in your house scares you to your marrow.

He picked up the food and dumped it on the kitchen table. *Eggs, cheese, herbs, hummus.* He cracked the eggs into the bowl, focussing on the procedure of mixing up an omelette. Forcing the image of his lips on hers out of his head.

He lit the gas and greased the pan. The beaten eggs sizzled as the mixture hit the heated surface. He reduced the heat.

'Good morning, Huon.'

He looked up and his chest tightened. Bronte stood in his kitchen, her hair cascading in a mass of curls around her shoulders. She wore one of his blue chambray casual shirts, which flowed across her rounded stomach but barely fell to mid-thigh.

She tugged self-consciously at the hem of the shirt. 'I can't seem to find my clothes.'

His gaze caught the action and travelled the length of her long, shapely legs and he imagined the soft mound at the top that was barely hidden underneath his shirt. His hand gripped the spatula.

'Huon?'

Her voice penetrated his fog of desire and he remembered the frying-pan. The omelette had just become scrambled eggs. 'Clothes, right. Sorry.' His brain had scrambled as well. 'I washed them for you and they're drying.'

Appreciation flashed through her eyes. 'Thanks.'

'No problem, I thought you'd feel more comfortable in your own clothes.' He grinned. 'Not that you don't look cute in my shirt.'

She tugged at the shirt again as if the action would lengthen it. Then she gave him a look of hurt mixed with disbelief. 'I feel ridiculous, and never in my life have I been cute.'

He wanted to shake his head in disbelief. How could she not know how gorgeous she was? She had no idea that she made his blood run so hot it almost boiled. That his fingers itched to touch her silky skin and explore the few areas the shirt actually covered.

He pulled out a chair. 'Here, everything will seem better after breakfast. I've made eggs.' He buttered toast, dished up the food, poured her tea, and sat down opposite her at the long red-gum table.

She leaned back in her chair with a devilish smile on her face.

'What?'

She waved her arm out in front of her across the top of the food. 'All of this from a man who eats at the pub most of the time.'

He laughed. 'Surprised I can cook? I used to cook a lot before Ellen died. But cooking for one isn't the same.'

'I agree, it's always easier to cook for more than one. Thanks for cooking for us.' She patted her tummy and smiled.

His stomach lurched. Since hearing the baby's heartbeat he could no longer just think of Bronte alone. It was now Bronte and the baby, inextricably entwined.

See, you enjoy cooking for them. The voice in his

head nagged and he tried to ignore it. She was a very temporary housemate.

Bronte started to eat then paused and fixed him with a long look. 'Living by yourself when you've been used to sharing a house can be really lonely. I imagine you've had some tough times.'

He thought of the long, quiet evenings, the nights he'd gone to the clinic or to the pub just to escape the stifling silence of the house. He nodded. 'The crazy thing is, when Ellen was alive she was often away on site at the gas fields. I didn't find the house quiet and oppressive then.'

'Because you knew she was coming home eventually.'

'Probably.'

'It's a funny thing, silence. It can be comforting. But when it's forced onto you, it can be scary, even soul-destroying.' She smiled a warm smile of understanding.

In a few short sentences she'd described exactly what it was like, living in his house. Why he'd left a lot of the house untouched and mainly lived in the kitchen area.

'Maybe you should get a dog. Pets are a great presence in a house.'

Huon almost choked on his eggs. 'What sort of pathetic message does that send? My wife dies and I get a dog.'

She tilted her head and looked straight at him. 'Ellen died two years ago, Huon.' Her matter-of-fact voice differed from what he was used to hearing when people spoke of Ellen.

Even so, he knew where this conversation was heading and he didn't want to go there. He got it often enough from Claire. 'Don't even think about telling me to move on. I'm quite happy with my life the way it is, and I have *no* plans to change it. Despite what most people think, not everyone in this world needs a partner.' The words rushed out in a forceful blast, stronger than he'd intended.

An understanding look crossed her face. 'I wouldn't presume to tell you it was time to get a partner, especially as my qualifications at coupledom are a dismal failure. But, Huon, it's not a crime to be lonely. Healthy human beings crave company. If you're not ready for a relationship, no one in this town would think less of you for getting a dog.'

He didn't want to hear this. Didn't want her understanding. Didn't want her knowing that the idea of loving someone else scared him to death. Didn't want her knowing he was lonely. Didn't want her knowing that last night, having her in the house had meant he'd slept well for the first time in months. 'I thought we were supposed to be organising you today, not me.'

She raised her brows and went back to eating her eggs.

His stomach suddenly didn't feel like food. He picked his plate up and walked to the sink. He didn't need to be analysed over breakfast. He was happy with his life the way it was and there was no way that he was putting himself out there again to be hurt. When you loved, you lost. He couldn't lose anyone again.

No, he didn't need to be analysed at all. Especially not by a glowing, pregnant woman. A woman with eyes that caressed him with concern, while wearing only his shirt.

Sexuality and sympathy. A potent mixture he had no idea how to handle.

He'd barely survived breakfast. The sooner he contacted the insurance company and Bronte was in her own house, the better. He wanted his quiet, unquestioning, non-probing house back.

Bronte ate the rest of her breakfast in silence. Perhaps she'd pushed Huon a bit far. Perhaps Claire's take on the situation wasn't accurate? His reaction when he'd thought she was going to tell him to move forward with his life had been very strong. Maybe he wasn't done grieving?

Ellen's touch was still very much part of the house unless Huon was into throw cushions and pastel furnishings. It didn't look like he'd changed much in two years. Except for the large kitchen. She could see Huon's stamp here.

It was a mish-mash of comfy furniture with state-of-the-art cookware. The large wooden table cried out for a crowd of people to gather around it, for children to crawl underneath it, and for food to make its surface groan.

But she wasn't sure Huon could recognise that just yet. She wished he could. Wished he could see that moving on was exactly what he did need. He would be happier if he did.

Women's voices sounded near the back door.

'Yoo-hoo, Huon.'

'In the kitchen.' Huon stowed the plate in the dishwasher.

Jenny Henderson walked in, carrying a large box, followed by Nancy Tigani, who clutched a bassinet, and Claire, who pushed a pram.

Claire gave Huon a motherly kiss. 'There's a load of stuff outside. Bring it in for us will you, dear?'

Huon raised his brows at being ordered about by his mother and gave her a mock salute. 'I'm on the job.'

As the wire door slammed behind him, the women put their load down on the table, looked at Bronte and all started to speak at the same time.

'Bronte, how are you? You poor thing.'

'What an awful thing to have happen to you.'

'At least you and the baby are all right. You are all right, aren't you?'

The concern in their voices swirled around her. 'Yes, the baby and I are fine. Homeless, but fine.'

Jenny gave her a hug. 'We know you lost everything. So last night after we heard the news we got on the blower and today we've got you some gear.' She pointed to some of the boxes. 'Baby clothes, pots and pans and we've also got some furniture.'

Bronte didn't know what to say. Words died on her tongue as a surge of emotion tightened her throat. 'That's so kind. I—'

'Nonsense, it's what we do when someone is having a hard time. After all, you've been looking after our families for the past few months, now it's our turn to look after you.' Jenny smiled and her voice filled with emotion. 'You kept me calm when Mark couldn't breathe. I'll never forget that.'

Tears stung the backs of Bronte's eyes. She went to speak, but Nancy sat down next to her and spoke first.

'And my Tom owes his life to you.' She squeezed Bronte's hand. 'We've got some clothes for you.

We're sorry they're not as trendy as those new maternity clothes you've been wearing just recently.' She looked over at Claire. 'Didn't she look just gorgeous in that vivid green dress that buttoned up the front? I loved it.'

Claire smiled. 'Actually, my favourite outfit was the striped cargo pants teamed with the ruched camisole top.'

Bronte had the weirdest feeling. It was very strange being discussed when she was present in the room. Kind of like an out-of-body experience.

Nancy turned back to Bronte and sighed. 'I always looked such a frump when I was pregnant. I wish I had your style.'

Bronte almost choked with shock. 'My style? I don't have any style. Now my sister, she got all the looks and style.'

Claire rolled her eyes. 'Bronte, believe me, you've got style and the looks. Since you got over your morning sickness and filled out, you've been glowing. And those vivid prints you chose work really well for you. Much better than that dull Melbourne-black-suit look you had when you arrived. You've created your own style and you look gorgeous. You just needed to come to Muttawindi to do it.'

Bronte looked at the women all nodding in agreement and wondered. No one had ever told her she was gorgeous. *You look pretty good to me*. A small voice whispered what Huon had said. But she hadn't listened.

Nancy smiled. 'Claire's right. And even though I couldn't wear these clothes with flair, I know you will.' A flicker of understanding crossed her face. 'I know it will feel very strange, wearing someone else's clothes, but it will only be for a week or so until you get can to Broken Hill or order up from Adelaide.'

Jenny got up and plugged in the kettle. 'And feel free to alter anything. I'm pretty handy with a needle so I'd be happy to do that for you. Nancy isn't going to need the clothes again, not since Greg's had the snip.'

Nancy giggled. 'Not unless I play up.'

The women laughed and Bronte sensed their strong bond of friendship. They had just extended part of that friendship to her.

Her heart soared. She may have lost her house, she may be wearing someone else's clothes for a bit, but these women cared about her situation enough to rally round her.

For the first time since coming to Muttawindi she had a glimpse of how it would be. Part of a town, part of a community. A doctor and a friend.

A box on legs staggered into the room. 'Hell, Mum, you've got enough stuff out there to fill the front room.' Huon wiped the sweat off his brow. He turned round and tripped over the pram.

'Ouch.' He pushed it out of the way with a shove and rubbed his shin.

Claire gave him a sanguine smile. 'Yes, well, you have plenty of room here so you won't notice it. I've told people to drop anything they have directly here. They can leave it on the veranda. Make sure you offer them a cup of tea if you're home.'

Bronte saw the look of horror on Huon's face at the realisation that his house was about to be filled with baby and house furniture. He was clearly regretting he'd asked her to stay. 'Claire, really, what you have brought here today is plenty…' Her voice trailed off as Claire fixed her with a steely look.

'This town looks after its own. You wouldn't want to offend anyone, would you?'

'No, I… No, certainly not.'

Claire smiled. 'Good, that's settled. Ron and I will be over later with another load.' She picked up her bag. 'Come on, ladies, we've got work to do.'

Jenny and Nancy gave Bronte a quick hug goodbye and one minute later the house was silent after the whirlwind.

Huon gave her a wry grin. 'I think you just got what you wanted. That was Muttawindi in action, the Muttawindi I knew you would eventually discover. They love nothing more than looking after someone who needs a hand.'

He picked up a box, his pants stretching taut across his behind. 'I'll move this into the front room. Then we'll ring Head Office and find you a new house.'

A chill sliced through the warm glow the women had brought her. She gave herself a shake. For so long she'd craved the acceptance of the town and now she had it.

So why did she have an empty space inside her? Suddenly she knew the love of the town was no longer enough. She wanted to be loved by a man. To be loved by a blue-eyed, blond-headed doctor who couldn't wait to move her out of his home.

The aching, empty space widened, and coldness seeped into every part of her.

* * *

'You need to take the medication every day, Mrs Chung.' Bronte tried hard not to let the frustration she felt show in her voice.

'I feel well. I fit, I take herbs.' The older Chinese woman spoke in a forthright manner.

'I understand that, but high blood pressure is called the silent killer for just that reason. You can feel well and then, wham, you have a stroke.' Bronte resorted to emotional blackmail. 'Look at Elsie Davis.'

'Ah. Very sad.' Mrs Chung's face softened. 'I miss her.'

'Everyone does.' Bronte covered Mrs Chung's work-worn hand. 'Keep exercising, keep taking your herbs but take your blood pressure medication as well, OK? I want you to be around and well enough to keep bringing me that sensational wonton soup.'

The older woman beamed. 'You need feeding. You want healthy baby. I put ginger in soup, helps digestion. Warm for baby. Baby close now.'

Bronte laughed. 'No, Mrs Chung, I still have quite a few weeks left to go.'

The old lady put her hand on Bronte's stomach and tilted her head to the side and grunted as if to say, *young girls know nothing*.

Bronte wrote up her notes after Mrs Chung had left. The town had thawed towards her so much that she now had to deal with many patients wanting to know how the pregnancy was going. This included them asking if they could feel her tummy.

There was something about pregnancy and the rest of the human race. No matter how bad things were, people's spirits seemed to be lifted by a pregnancy and the thought of a new life.

A few of the older patients had initially tut-tutted about the lack of a husband, but most people seemed to be accepting of her as a sole parent. This baby was going to have an entire town of honorary aunts and uncles.

Bronte stretched and rubbed her back.

'Knock, knock. Got a minute?'

She turned towards the door. Huon stood in the doorway, holding two steaming mugs. He looked like a grown-up version of a rough-and-tumble boy with his blond hair curling up on his collar, his cowlick springing forward, resisting all efforts to be flattened, and his clothes looking like they'd been thrown on.

Given that he'd been out to an early morning emergency, they probably had been. She'd heard his footsteps on the Baltic pine floorboards at about five a.m.

'Sure, what's up?'

'Lewis Barkly's in Coronary Care at Broken Hill. Apparently he'd stopped taking his beta blocker medication and now he has unstable angina.' Huon sighed. 'These old miners think they're as tough as old boots. I just wish they'd listen to me more.'

'I just had Mrs Chung in with failure to comply as well. I think I need to start a group for these elderly patients. They can get together and I can give a quick chat about general health, answer questions about medication, and then they can have a chinwag for the rest of the time.'

Huon laughed a deep rumbling laugh and his eyes twinkled. 'Great idea, but you're just doing it because you know Mavis Petrie will arrive with one of her triple sponge cakes, and Mrs Chung will bring you more soup.'

'Absolutely! You know me too well.' Bronte forced herself to ignore the flare of longing that rocked her body whenever Huon smiled at her. She had to ignore it or she would fall apart. 'Actually, I was planning on that soup being my contribution to dinner tonight.'

He laughed. 'Copping out on cooking again?'

'Not at all.' She tried to look affronted, without success.

Sharing the evening meal with Huon had become the highlight of her day. Technically they took it in turns to cook, but she'd noticed he often arrived home before her and started the meal. He would urge her to lie on the couch and chat to him while he cooked. The conversation would start off as patient debriefs, but would soon range over a broad range of subjects.

She so enjoyed this time and she knew life would be lonely when she finally moved into her house.

Huon's voice broke into her thoughts. 'But, seriously, a group for the elderly is a good idea. Perhaps you could start it before you go on maternity leave and I can run it while you're away?'

'I can start the group and manage it while I'm on leave.'

'Just wait and see how you go, OK?'

His concern wrapped around her and she wanted to sink into it, but there was no point. He was a kind, considerate boss, a caring friend, but nothing more. She had to learn to be content with friendship. Had he felt more than friendship for her, he wouldn't be harassing the insurance company so much to get her moved out of his house.

Huon pulled a printed piece of card out of his shirt

pocket and turned it over a few times in his hand. Then he slapped it on his thigh.

Bronte looked from his face to the card and back again. A range of emotions played over his ruggedly, handsome face. Then he ran his hand through his hair.

'What do you need to tell me?' Bronte gave him a direct look.

Huon looked sheepish. 'Why do you think I need to tell you something?'

Bronte smiled. 'The hand-through-the-hair thing.'

'What?'

'Whenever you're worried about something or needing to do something you don't want to do, you run your hand through your hair.'

He looked at her surprised. 'Really? Do I? I had no idea.'

She laughed at his baffled expression. 'Well, you do, so spill the beans.'

'You know how our organization has to do a lot of fundraising to keep our planes in the air?'

'Yes. Claire gave me a run-down the other day when we were in Broken Hill. She also introduced me to the very formidable Catherine Berry. Within ten minutes she had me buying and posting a soft toy plane to every child I knew.' Bronte giggled at the memory.

'We need more Catherines.' Huon grinned. 'If it makes you feel any better, she has me organised every year with an ever-increasing number of Christmas cards. Unfortunately she doesn't offer to write and send them for me, so most are in my bottom drawer at home.

'Anyway, our region has a huge fundraising effort

each year, culminating in the Outback Ball. People fly in from all over New South Wales and southern Queensland. It's a sensational weekend, loads of fun.'

Bronte grimaced. 'I guess it is, if you enjoy that sort of thing. Even before the debacle of Damien, I never enjoyed the glittering social scene.'

He gave her a sympathetic smile. 'I know the full-catastrophe social occasion is not your thing, especially after your experience at your last ball, but this will be different and you'll have a great time.'

Bronte's mouth went dry at the thought of a crowd, a ball and dancing. 'No, I won't have a great time. I left Melbourne to get away from all of that stuff. Besides, someone has to stay behind to attend any emergencies and that suits me. You go and I'll man the fort.'

'Sorry, Bronte. You have to come. The community will expect it. It's all part of the job.'

She crossed her arms across her chest. 'No, my job is to be their doctor, not their social butterfly. I'm sorry, Huon, but the community will have to accept that I can't be there. I do much better meeting people one on one.'

'It's part of your job description.'

His words numbed her. 'What?'

'As a Muttawindi flying doctor, you're expected to take part in fundraising activities. This goes with the territory.'

Oh, God. Panic started to rise in her chest. She had no choice. Just like with her family. Duty.

Her voice croaked on the words. 'When is it?'

'Tomorrow.'

'Tomorrow!' Her head spun. 'I can't go. I don't have

a dress. I'm seven months pregnant, for heaven's sake, and even Broken Hill wouldn't have the sort of dress I'd need.'

A shaft of rational thought pierced her panic. She narrowed her frantic gaze at Huon. 'How long have you known about this?'

Colour stained his cheeks. 'Six weeks.'

'Six weeks!' Her voice rose hysterically. 'Why didn't you tell me?'

'Because I knew you'd react like this. Because your house burnt down. But mostly because the last ball you went to wasn't a good experience for you.' He put his hand on hers. 'But this is work, Bronte. Remember that. Plus the people of the district here value you. You know that now.'

The heat of his hand seeped into her. Her head spun, her chest tightened. A ball. Dear God, she couldn't do it. Couldn't walk into the crowd pregnant, dowdy and alone.

But before she could speak, Huon stood up and walked out into the corridor. A moment later he returned, carrying a large box with a well-known designer's logo printed on the top.

He placed it down in front of her. 'The dress problem is solved. I ordered this for you and it came in on yesterday's mail plane.' His eyes crinkled at the edges.

Bronte sat stunned. A million thoughts raced across her brain, going in all directions, never stopping long enough to form.

Huon put his hand on her shoulder. 'I'll be there with you the whole time. It'll be OK, Bronte, I promise.'

She looked up into his face. His expression was of concern mixed with expectation. She faced defeat. No matter how much she wanted to, she couldn't wriggle out of this. She sighed. 'Where's the ball?'

'This year it's at the Lundgreens' Station, which is an hour's flight away. We'll head off after morning clinic tomorrow and stay the night at the station.' He stood up and smiled down at her, his dimples carving deep into his face, giving him a devilish look. 'Remember to pack the dress.'

He walked out of the office.

A kernel of anger flared inside Bronte. How could he have withheld the information about the ball from her? The whole town had left her out of the loop, as if they had all conspired against her to get her there.

She felt powerless, and she hated that. Huon had organised everything and she was expected to just tag along. Just like at home. Just like her parents.

She dumped the dress box onto the floor without opening it. She wanted to kick something. She wanted to hit something.

She wanted to cry.

Except this situation wasn't quite the same as with her parents. She glanced down at the dress box. This large rectangular box represented a wonderfully kind man. A man who had not only listened to her but had taken on board what she had said all those weeks ago.

Curiosity overcame her. She leaned over, opened the lid and gingerly pulled back the layers of pale blue tissue paper.

She gasped. Her fingers touched silver-grey silk. The bodice was covered in tiny grey, blue and white beads. She pulled the dress out of the box and held it up against her. Full length and sleeveless, with a short fitted bodice and masses of flowing silk to cascade over the baby, it was the most elegant gown she'd ever owned. But she wouldn't be able to do justice to the dress. Beautiful women wore dresses like this. Not her.

I'll be there with you the whole time. It will be OK, Bronte, I promise. Huon's words echoed in her head.

Yes, he'd be there as her boss and her friend, just like he always was. Dealing with that when she wanted so much more was harder than the thought of the ball itself.

She rubbed her stomach. 'Well, baby, looks like we're going to a ball. Let's hope the plane holds up better than the pumpkin.'

CHAPTER NINE

HER HEART POUNDED, her fingers trembled and a wave of stress-induced heat swamped her. Bronte dragged in a deep, calming breath. There was no way she was going to sweat on this gorgeous dress. She slipped her feet into delicate silver sandals, brushed on some pearly pink lipstick and spritzed her favourite perfume onto her neck and wrists.

The day had seemed interminable. She'd stretched out morning clinic as long as possible, until Huon had pulled rank and ordered her onto the plane. Normally she loved to sit and gaze out of the plane window at the expanse of red dust and grey scrub, taking advantage of a trip that wasn't a medical emergency. But today the landscape had passed in a blur.

In stark contrast to the entire district, she was the only person not caught up in the excitement of the event. At the clinic, all her elderly patients had excitedly asked her about the ball and said how much she must be looking forward to it. They had insisted she give them a blow-by-blow description next week.

Mrs Nikvolski had given her a knowing look and in

her fractured English had said, 'Dr Morrison, he look good in a tuxedo, yes.'

Bronte knew he would look more than good. Part of her ached to see him, another part didn't want that painful frustration. Wanting so much more than friendship and knowing it wasn't on offer, cut her deeper every day.

The whole occasion filled her with dread. Snatches of the last ball she'd attended kept rolling across her brain. Damien's voice snarled in her head, *There wasn't anything left in the looks department for you after Stephanie took it all.*

She gave herself a shake to try and rid herself of the negative thoughts that plagued her. She was here. Huon was with her. She would get through this.

The room the Lundgreens had given her to dress in had a full-length mirror. Up until then she'd avoided looking at herself in the dress, but it was crunch time. Any minute Huon would collect her to walk her down to the ballroom.

The baby somersaulted inside her. 'OK kid, I'm going to open my eyes any second and look.'

She'd never taken so long over make-up, never spent this amount of time on her hair. But the dress demanded perfection and although she knew she fell a long way short of that, she didn't want to look like a pregnant whale either.

'Five, four, three…'

The baby kicked her.

'Oh, all right.' Bronte went to open her eyes as a knock sounded on the door. She spun away from the mirror, her heart beating out an erratic rhythm. Huon had arrived.

She pulled the door open. Her breath stalled. He stood in front of her, all six feet of him, clothed in an immaculate black tuxedo that fitted him like a glove.

The pin-tucks on his white shirt lay crisp and sharp against his solid chest and flat stomach. Perfection from head to toe, except for his bow-tie, which lay untied around his neck. A grey piece of silk, dark against the whiteness of his shirt.

She wanted to savour this moment before words intruded, before she lost him to the other women at the ball. She wanted to memorise the image of this handsome man. The way his blond hair curled, how his bluest-of-blue eyes twinkled with easy humour, and how his tanned face, now free of the shadows of fatigue, relaxed into a deep dimpled smile that took her breath away. And had done from the very first moment she'd met him.

'Bronte.' Huon's deep voice broke into her concentration. 'You look amazing.'

She glanced down at her dress and back at him, disbelief and uncertainty filling her. He was only being polite. She sighed. 'You don't have to say that.'

Frustration crossed his face. 'What are you talking about? Haven't you seen yourself in the mirror?'

She dropped her gaze from his probing look. He knew her too well.

'Damn it, Bronte, you haven't looked, have you?'

'I was about to when you—'

Without waiting for her to finish her sentence, he grabbed her hand, swung her out behind him and then frog-marched her back into the room and over to the mirror.

'Look, damn it.' His hand held hers firmly.

'You're as bad as the baby,' she mumbled under her breath.

'What?' Confusion underlined his frustration.

'Nothing. I'm looking, I'm looking.' Her heart pounded so hard she was sure he must hear it.

She slowly raised her gaze to the mirror. And blinked. Twice. She hardly recognised herself. The silver-grey of the dress made her eyes large and luminous. The flowing material flattered her pregnancy and for the first time ever the bodice hinted at a cleavage.

Huon spoke softly. 'You look stunning. Surely you can see that?' He gripped her hand securely. 'And men like Damien are not worth thinking about.' He looked at her, his eyes willing her to really listen. 'Forget him, he's not worth your concern. People like him wouldn't know true beauty if it kicked them.'

She wanted to believe him but still the voices of her family filled her head.

His voice deepened. 'You've always been gorgeous, you just didn't recognise it.'

His words called up other words. *I wish I had your style*. Nancy Tigani's voice sounded in her head, along with that of Jenny Henderson and some of her other patients. Bronte looked in the mirror again.

A new thought slowly emerged, putting down tentative roots. Perhaps she did have style? It was certainly a different style from Stephanie's and her mother's, but it was *her* style. The thoughts fired up. And her style looked pretty good. Lightness flooded her. She was an attractive woman in her own right. Stephanie had classic good looks, but beauty came in different packages.

And Huon had seen it. Her heart turned over. He'd recognised her style when he'd chosen this dress. Her heart ached with gratitude. He'd seen something in her that she'd never seen before. And he cared enough to want her to see it.

She suddenly realised he'd been edging her gently towards this moment. He'd seen what she'd been blind to all her life.

This amazing man who held her hand had opened her eyes, infusing her with self-confidence. He'd given her a gift no one else had, and she loved him for it.

She loved him.

She raised her eyes to his reflection as the realisation hit her. She loved him. For too long she'd tried to tell herself it was a crush, a silly infatuation. But she knew it was much more than that. This wonderful man was her closest friend, her confidant and her mentor. He was the first person she thought of in the morning and the last person she thought of at night. He filled her thoughts and dreams.

But he didn't love her.

And he couldn't know how she felt. Somehow she had to keep the knowledge of her love for him to herself. Tonight, tomorrow and for ever.

Huon studied Bronte's expression anxiously. She'd been silent for a few moments and had schooled her emotions into a blank mask. He couldn't tell what she was thinking about the dress, herself, anything.

Suddenly she smiled, smoothed the silk over the baby and turned towards him. 'Thanks for the dress, Huon. You're right, it's just my style.'

Relief flooded him. 'It's my very great pleasure.'

The dress had been a big leap but worth it. He'd been racking his brain for weeks about how to open Bronte's eyes to her own loveliness.

He didn't know why it had become so important to him that she see this in herself. And he didn't want to examine those feelings too closely. Now was the time to enjoy the evening with a beautiful woman on his arm.

He let go of her hand and crooked his arm out towards her. 'Shall we go to the ball?'

'I don't think so.'

His stomach dropped and he scanned her face. 'What's the problem?'

Her eyes flashed with devilment. 'This dress and I deserve an escort who is fully dressed.'

Relief filled him and he laughed. 'Bow-ties and I don't go together very well.'

She rolled her eyes. 'So you can manage tiny stitches when little Julie Mondale cut her eye, but you can't tie a bow-tie.'

'Guilty as charged.' He grinned ruefully.

'I'll do it for you.' She stepped forward and picked up the ends of the bow-tie. Her hair brushed his face and her spicy perfume enveloped him as her fingers gently brushed his neck.

Her head down bent, her focus completely on the job

in hand, she had no idea what she was doing to him. Like a flame to fireworks, her touch set off explosions of longing deep inside him. His groin tightened.

This bow-tying was a bad idea.

He'd spent a lot of time in the last few weeks avoiding being alone with Bronte in his house. To avoid this sort of closeness. The sort of closeness that battered him and tossed his emotions around like a dinghy on the ocean.

But he'd promised Bronte he'd escort her to the ball and make sure she had a good time. And that was what he was going to do, no matter how tough he found it to stay detached. She deserved this night. A night where, for the first time, she could walk into a room with confidence in herself and shine.

'There you go, that was easy.' She stood back and cool air raced between them, filling the space that had a moment ago glowed white with heat. She smiled up expectantly at him. 'The hard bit's over. Now we can go to the ball.'

But the hardest part of the evening was just beginning.

Bronte was having the most wonderful time. She'd never been to a ball quite like it and she'd danced until she was breathless. The night sky glowed with a canopy of stars that only the outback could offer. The dance floor, half inside the marquee and half outside, gave a romance to the night no big city venue could match.

Fresh seafood had been flown in for the occasion, piled high on ice, and Bronte realised there was *one* thing she did miss about Melbourne.

She'd danced with Brendan, Greg, and even with

Ben, who, complete with pressure bandages on his burns, had made his first outing since coming home from Adelaide.

She sipped her lemonade. She belonged to this fantastic community. They valued her and welcomed her. Life was good.

But her gaze kept straying to Huon. Across the room she saw him dancing with Hayley Gaylard. A stab of jealousy ripped through her.

Huon saw her and waved, his grin melting her bones.

He had no idea the pain his *bonhomie* caused her. He'd been attentive all evening, making sure she had a drink, that she wasn't too tired. Being the friend he had always been. Nothing more, nothing less.

And why should she expect anything else? She might love him but he'd made it clear he wasn't ready for a partner. He, too, had fears he was fighting.

Even if he overcame those fears, would he want her? She didn't know. But she did know one thing. Tonight she felt beautiful. Tonight she glowed, and Huon had seen that.

'Ladies and gentlemen, take your partners for the final dance set.' The master of ceremony's voice boomed out of the large black speakers.

'May I have this dance?' Huon appeared beside her, his face mock serious, his hand extended.

She laughed and bowed. 'My card has one vacancy.'

'Glad to hear it! You've been a hard woman to catch.' His eyes danced with fun.

'That's what happens when you do a *Pygmalion* number on a girl.'

His eyes went serious for a moment. 'You did that all on your own. A dress is just window-dressing. When you glow from the inside, people warm to that.'

Everyone but you.

'Come on, they're playing our song.' He pulled her out on the dance floor and spun her around to the well-known 1970s tune.

Laughter and elation filled her as her body moved to the music, swaying to the beat. As she spun, she glimpsed Huon's warm, smiling face, his cheeky grin and look of relaxed happiness. It was a far cry from the exhausted man who'd met her at Broken Hill six months ago. Had she been part of that change?

Just when she thought she would never catch her breath, the beat changed.

Huon drew her in tenderly, as if in slow motion. His arm circling her waist, gently pressing her ever closer to him until her belly touched him. His chest pressed against hers. His heart beat against her breast hard and fast, just like her own.

The familiar heat from his touch surged inside her. Time slowed down. Every moment extended. Every moment intensified. The music wrapped around her, drawing her closer to Huon. Narrowing her world, this time, this moment to Huon and nothing else.

His fingers tightened on hers. His head moved nearer, his smooth cheek brushing hers in a soft caress.

Tiny sparks erupted, racing through her, touching all parts of her. She swayed towards him, as if pulled by a gossamer thread. Any space between them was too big.

The length of his body moved against hers, moulding into her curves, around the baby, as if he was designed to fit to her. As if together they had found their rightful places.

His heat transferred into her body, tantalising her with longing, yet confirming that they belonged together.

This was different to anything she'd ever experienced. This time she knew with a clarity that stunned her. This was her man and she wanted him.

Her gaze sought his. The shutters he normally kept tightly battened on his emotions rose for a moment and she glimpsed wanting, longing and desire.

Wanting, longing and desire for her.

Her heart soared. He wanted her. Sure, he was fighting wanting her, but he did have real feelings that matched her own.

Wordlessly they danced out under the night sky, their eyes never breaking contact, messages of need shifting between them, powerful and primal.

The other couples receded into the background. Bronte was only aware of Huon, the touch of his breath on her face, the heat of his body against her, the caress of his hand on her back and the driving need to feel him even more closely.

She needed to show him he could love again. That he didn't need to fear the longing. That it was OK to go with the overwhelming attraction and give in to the desire. Show him that his fears belonged in the past.

Tonight she was beautiful. Tonight she could do this.

Her foot pivoted on the edge of the dance floor. The house was only metres away. 'Come on.' She whispered the words as she gently pulled him towards the house.

He hesitated for a moment. 'Bronte, this isn't a good idea. I—'

She put her finger to his lips. 'Shh. Stop thinking, just go with the flow.'

His eyes darkened with desire, but flickered with a kernel of restraint.

The restraint worried her. She leaned towards him and ran her tongue slowly along his bottom lip, imprinting herself onto him. Branding him, making him hers.

The restraint in his eyes withered as desire flared. He groaned and followed her to the house. They slowly made their way to the bedroom, closing the door firmly behind them. Worry etched his brow. 'Bronte, you're killing me. Are you *really* sure about this?'

'I'm very sure.' She stepped into his arms, wrapping them around her. 'This is meant to be. We've fought it long enough. Take a chance, take a chance at happiness.'

He stood still, looking at her, his deep blue gaze penetrating her soul. A war of emotions swirled in his eyes—yearning, self-control, fear and lust.

She couldn't breathe. What if he rejected her? What if he threw away this chance?

He sighed a long shuddering breath, as if all the restraint he'd placed on his emotions had suddenly broken loose. He lowered his head and captured her lips with his.

Elation surged through her. He tasted of champagne, strawberries and wonder. She welcomed him, knowing that he belonged to her, sealing him to her with her own heat and taste.

His hands released her hair and he buried his face in it, a small moan escaping his lips.

She gloried that she could do this to him. She ran her hand through his curls and down along his neck, releasing the bow-tie she'd so carefully tied a few short hours ago. She longed to have his skin against hers, to touch his solid chest and taste the saltiness of his body.

His lips found her neck and she arched back, giving him free access to explore, taste and tantalise.

With one hand he eased the zip of her frock, which fell to the floor. For a brief moment panic flared that he would not like what he saw. But he stood before her, his eyes full of awe, marvelling at the pregnant swell of her body.

He reverently rested his hand on her belly. 'If you're worried, we don't have to…' His voice trailed off.

She cupped her hand around his face, in awe of the thoughtfulness of this amazing man, who put her needs ahead of his. 'The baby and I are just fine. We want you.'

She slid off his shirt and pressed her lips to his chest, flicking her tongue across his nipples.

He groaned and pulled her gently down onto the bed. 'I think it's my turn to do some exploring.'

And he did. Using his tongue in ways she never thought possible, he traversed her body. He caressed her nipples, sending ribbons of pleasure rocking through her. He trailed his lips across her belly, igniting a path of wanting, winding lower and lower until she was a quivering mess, urgent with need, clamouring for release.

But still he wouldn't let her go.

'We're doing this together, sweetheart.' His gentleness brought tears to her eyes as he eased inside her, the ultimate transfer of heat.

She moaned with the wonder of feeling him in the

truest sense, nothing between them but white-hot desire overlaid with loving.

Slowly, gently and with reverence he stroked her, building her need, taking her with him, climbing to the place where they belonged. Joy, pure and wondrous, surged inside her as together they flew.

Later, Bronte lay in Huon's arms sated and secure, knowing she belonged here. She revelled in the comfort and protection of his strong arms and the sense of finally coming to a true home.

She'd found her true love and the knowledge filled her with a bliss she'd never thought a person could know.

Huon felt the regular swoosh of Bronte's breath against his chest. He lay and watched her sleep. Her long lashes caressed her cheeks, and her plump, ruby lips, which had so recently caused him so much pleasure, were slightly parted.

He let himself just watch her, releasing his mind to wander in a euphoric daze, flitting from thought to thought.

It had been so long since he'd lain with a woman and his body still tingled in awe at the sensations she had elicited.

He had never imagined that tonight he would make love to Bronte. He'd been alone for too long. For months he'd fought his attraction to this sexy, courageous woman. Tonight, when she'd so generously given herself to him, he'd given in to desire and taken what she offered.

His plan of keeping some distance hadn't worked. He thought he'd be safe if he danced with the nurses, the mothers and the grandmothers, but he'd always known exactly where Bronte had been in the marquee.

Every time he'd seen her dancing in another man's arms he'd wanted to cut in. Whenever she'd laughed, smiled and unconsciously twirled a lose strand of hair around her finger as she'd talked to the young station hands, he'd wanted to storm over and claim her as his.

And finally when he'd held her in his arms on the dance floor and she'd looked up at him with her large eyes, darkened with desire, he'd fallen into their depths. He'd tried to hold onto his resolve, but hell, didn't he deserve to be in the arms of a gorgeous woman if she wanted him?

Happiness and contentment permeated every cell of his body. *Take a chance at happiness*. Bronte's words played across his mind. Perhaps she was right.

Bronte, the baby and me. The thought swirled in his head. A house, kids in the yard, a wife, colleague and lover all rolled into one. Other people lived the dream, and he could, too. Why had he fought it for so long?

Bronte snuggled into him, a sigh escaping her lips, her hand splayed against his chest in a proprietorial way.

The euphoric haze vaporised.

Reality cascaded over him like a bucket of icy water.

Panic made him rigid. Dear God, what had he done? He'd made love to Bronte. Pregnant Bronte, colleague Bronte, dear friend Bronte. A woman who'd been so hurt before she would only have given herself to him because she loved him.

He couldn't be that man.

He couldn't be anyone's partner ever again.

He'd barely survived losing his parents and Ellen. And Bronte came with a baby. A child who would wrap itself around his heart like vines in a jungle. Tight, unconditional, unyielding.

He'd opened his heart as a youth to Ellen and had lost part of it when she'd died. Now he was all grown up and knew the danger of loving. Losing Bronte and her child would be double the pain and he would go under. Grief would consume him.

He had to walk away now. Walk away before he loved her. Walk away while it was still just lust. It was better to be alone than destroyed by grief. The last two years had taught him that.

He had the town to care for, and they cared for him. It was a safe life. It had to be enough.

CHAPTER TEN

BRONTE LAY NEXT to Huon, revelling in his warmth and comfort. They'd made love. She'd convinced him to take a chance at happiness, to put his fear aside. Now they could both move forward with their lives.

Move forward together. Together with a baby.

She snuggled in, wrapping her legs around his.

Huon suddenly stiffened against her.

She lessened the pressure against his leg. 'Sorry, did I hurt you?'

'No.' He moved away from her slightly.

Bronte squashed the jab of disappointment that edged in under her ribs.

The mattress moved and Huon swung his legs over the edge of the bed, sitting up with his back to her.

Cold swooped in, chilling her skin. Chilling her inside and out. She struggled to think clearly. Something was very wrong.

Huon cleared his throat. 'I think I'd better head back to my room. We wouldn't want to embarrass the Lundgreens.'

She sat up, pulling the sheet around her, suddenly

self-conscious about her nakedness. She finally found her voice and spoke against the rising panic that threatened to choke her. 'I think the Lundgreens probably expected things like this to happen.'

Huon stood up and pulled on his trousers. 'We're the local doctors so we need to act with some decorum, don't you think?' The zip of his trousers sounded loud against the booming silence in the room.

'I think we need to talk about what's going on here.'

He bent to tie his shoes, deliberately not looking at her. 'Nothing is going on here. I have to work in the morning so I'm going to my room to get some sleep.'

Bile scalded her throat. Her heart beat so fast she thought she might faint. She gripped the sheet to her chin and frantically tried to stay on top of her world, which had suddenly tipped sideways. Huon was leaving her.

It had happened again. She'd been duped by a man. Used and discarded. She blinked back the tears that stung her eyes. She would not cry in front of him. She would hold onto her dignity.

No! A voice screamed in her head. This wasn't like Damien. She felt the difference but struggled to work out what is was.

Her thoughts raced around her head as she tried to absorb and make sense of Huon's rejection of her. A few short hours ago she'd believed he was finally over Ellen. Believed he was ready to take a risk and move on with his life, despite what he'd once said about living alone. And she'd pushed him to take that risk.

She'd fallen in love with a kind, generous, caring

man. A man who, despite the personal losses in his life, still managed to care for others ahead of himself.

She bit her lip and breathed deeply. But was he caring for himself? Memories of a conversation with Claire flashed across her mind.

It's hard, watching him put his life on pause. He'd make a great father. He and Ellen had planned to have children. He needs someone to show him he's ready.

Suddenly she knew his rejection of her wasn't anything to do with her. It wasn't because she was a poor second to anyone. It had nothing to do with her looks.

It had everything to do with him putting his life on pause. Treading water. Not risking love again. He'd loved and lost his parents, he'd loved and lost Ellen. He was scared of losing her so he was sending her away.

Pain now, less pain later. Crazy thinking. How did she fight that? 'We've just made love. You can't deny how wonderful it was for both of us.'

His eyes, dull with resignation, sought hers. 'Bronte, I… Look… I'm sorry. I should never have given in to you. One of us should have been sensible. It should never have happened.'

'But it *did* happen.' *Because I love you.* She tried to keep her voice level. 'It happened because of an overwhelming attraction between two consenting adults. An attraction we've both fought for a long time.'

'We should have kept fighting it.' He ran his hand through his hair in a familiar gesture. 'We made a mistake.'

Frustration surged inside her. 'No, *we* didn't make a mistake. I know that *I* made the right decision.'

'OK, *I* made a mistake and, heaven knows, I'm truly

sorry. But this isn't meant to be. You're not ready for this. Right now you need to be focussing on your baby.'

Disbelief rocked her. 'Don't presume to tell me what I am or am not ready for. Look at yourself. You're the one pushing me away. You're the one not ready.'

'I can't give you what you want.' His voice, ragged with guilt, sliced through her.

Her heart contracted in pain. 'What do you think I want?'

'You want someone to love you. You want a lover, a husband and a father for your child.'

The words, stark and harsh, pummelled her, shaking her resolve that she could fight his false belief. Lover, husband and father to her child were exactly what she wanted.

And that was exactly what he was running from.

Her face paled even more. 'Hell, Bronte, I didn't mean to hurt you.'

'It's a bit late for that now. The damage is done.' Her words, edged with steel, cut deep.

He wanted to make her pain less but he didn't know how. 'I tried being married once.' The words sounded trite.

'And by all accounts you had a happy marriage. You could have that again.'

'I had a short marriage. I can't do that again.'

'You're choosing not to do it again, Huon. You're choosing to put your life in neutral, commit to no one and deny yourself any chance of happiness.'

His heart twisted as her words struck deeply. 'You don't understand, no one really understands—'

She cut across his words. 'I think I *do* understand. No one can predict the future, Huon, but avoiding relationships just in case they don't work out, or get cut short, isn't living.'

'It's worked well for the last two years.' He held onto those words, ignoring the disbelieving voices in his head.

Bronte's derisive look screamed that he was a coward.

'What? Working yourself so hard so you can't even think or feel? Being on call to the town so you can kid yourself that their care and devotion is enough to sustain you emotionally?'

Her words bombarded him like shrapnel. He needed to cut this conversation off. Fast. 'I'm sorry I've hurt you, but as a couple and a family we were never going to work out.'

'That's right.' The bitterness in her voice ate at him like acid on paper. 'We wouldn't work out because you won't even try.'

She hauled in a deep breath. 'I'm not begging for your love, Huon. I deserve better than that. But you're throwing away a chance at happiness. A real chance to restart your life, a life lived to the full instead of this half-life you're clinging to now.'

She got up from the bed and grabbed her dressing-gown, pulling the sash tightly around her. 'As soon as I get back to Muttawindi, I'll move into the pub. I don't want to impose on you any longer.'

He sighed. 'Don't be ridiculous. Stay until your house is ready. We're both adults. Surely we can be civilised and share a house for a few more days.'

'That's right, we're adults.' She spoke firmly, with no trace of emotion. 'Just like you, I'm making a choice. And I'm choosing *not* to live in your house a moment longer than I have to.'

She marched to the door and hauled it open. 'I'm ready for you to leave now.' She looked at him, her head tilted to one side, her hair gently falling around her face. He experienced the ever-strengthening tug on his feelings, which he tried to stop.

He walked towards the door. His gut ached, his head pounded, and so did his heart. He'd done what he'd had to do. Bronte was under no illusions of a happy-ever-after. And he was getting his old life back.

So why did it feel so wrong?

'Landing in two minutes, Bronte.' Brendan's voice sounded in her headphones.

Rain pounded the plane windows and a wave of apprehension gripped her. She hoped the storm would pass quickly because rain could turn outback airstrips into quagmires in a very short time.

'Helen's symptoms sound very much like appendicitis. And with this weather, let's make it a quick evacuation. None of us fancy being stranded at Nandana, doing emergency surgery.' Claire voiced Bronte's thoughts.

She nodded in agreement and rubbed the slight dragging pain on her abdomen. The baby must be pressing on something. Probably ligament pain.

'You OK?' Claire had been trying to mother Bronte over the long seven days since the ball.

'Fine.' But she wasn't fine. She was physically exhausted and emotionally numb. Work had been frantic but she'd welcomed the diversion it had offered. During the day she had focus. It was the long, lonely, empty nights she hated.

She hadn't moved into the pub as the insurance company had come through with her house. Technically, she had moved into her new home. The boxes stacked high were testament to that. Claire and Nancy had fussed about, offering to unpack for her, but right now she couldn't face it. So she got up each morning, went to work, came home and went to bed.

She knew she needed to focus on the baby. Knew she needed to get her house ready, do some nesting. But she couldn't bring herself to start.

Each day she saw the worry in her patients' eyes. Worry for herself, worry that their town might lose one or both of their doctors. She knew she looked grey and gaunt. No one had really said anything specific, but people knew. Knew she loved Huon. Knew he didn't love her.

They squeezed her arm; they touched her hand and shook their heads. It took every ounce of energy she had to hold herself together.

She'd momentarily toyed with the idea of leaving. But she wasn't leaving. This was her town now. She'd worked too hard to run away. Worked too hard to prove to her parents she could stand on her own feet and live her own life. They'd finally accepted that and as a peace offering had sent her a cot for the baby.

The sun would rise and set each day, but her life would never be the same. But she would get through it. Somehow.

Huon had taken leave and gone to a conference in Sydney. She had seven days before she had to face him. A week to pull herself together. A week to learn how to turn the clock back, and be his colleague again instead of his lover.

A week to learn how to cope with loving a man who couldn't love her back.

The plane's undercarriage vibrated and the wheels touched the ground roughly. Not Brendan's usual smooth landing, so the strip conditions were already changing.

A frantic Barry Pappas met the plane, his rain jacket soaked through. 'Bronte, she's just collapsed.'

'Let's go!' Bronte jumped into the truck, her medical case banging her legs. The dull pain in her stomach turned sharp for a brief moment. She grimaced and gripped the handlebar above the window.

The pain faded.

Barry raced the truck through every pothole on the gravel track. The vehicle had barely stopped when Bronte opened the door. The rain slashed at her as she ran the short distance to the back door of the homestead.

'Doctor, she's in here.' Jane Pappas's terrified voice called from down the corridor. 'She keeps going to sleep on me.'

Bronte knelt down next to Helen. She gave Helen's shoulder a shake.

Helen groaned and her eyes fluttered open and then closed.

'Well done, Jane, for putting her in coma position.' Bronte gave the scared teenager a reassuring smile. Then she did the ABC of emergency care. Helen's airway was clear, but her breathing was too rapid.

Claire took Helen's blood pressure. 'Eighty over forty.'

Shock had lowered her blood pressure but was it due to a bleed or peritonitis? 'Tell me what Mum said about where it hurt.'

'She hadn't felt well for a few days. She had a pain but it moved about a bit. But she was gripping her tummy when she fell. She'd been vomiting this horrid brown stuff.' The young woman's face blanched at the description.

'Her temperature is 40.' The thermometer beeped in Claire's hand.

'Barry, is Helen allergic to penicillin?'

'No.' The farmer's face was white under his tan.

'I'll put in an IV. Claire, you draw up penicillin and then put in a second IV. We need to get a jump on this infection.'

Claire had already got out the antibiotics. Bronte appreciated her knowledge and experience. But she missed Huon. When Huon was with her, the load seemed shared.

Now everyone's expectations rested on her shoulders.

And she had a desperately sick woman spiralling into hypovolaemic shock.

'Bronte.' Brendan's deep voice, laced with urgency, made her turn.

'You've got five minutes or we won't be able to get out. The strip is turning into mud.'

'Right.' Hell, just what they didn't need. She wanted a stable patient before they were airborne, but if they were stuck at Nandana, Helen would die.

A jagged pain pierced her. Instinctively she put her hand on her lower belly, which felt hard under her fingers. She breathed out. The pain receded.

She focussed on Helen. Her veins had collapsed due to shock and finding a site for the IV was like looking for a needle in a haystack. She tightened the tourniquet. 'Claire, have you found a vein?'

'Still trying.' Unease made her voice quaver.

Bronte's finger's gently palpated Helen's skin.

'Three minutes, Bronte!'

Brendan's words hammered at her. She dragged in a calming breath. She would find a vein. *Must* find a vein. A small mound rose under her fingers. She flicked off the cannula cover and slid the needle home. 'Gotcha.'

'I've got a vein in her foot.' Claire inserted the needle and drew back blood. 'Thank goodness.' The relief in her voice echoed Bronte's.

'Brendan, we're ready. On my count.'

Barry and Brendan stepped forward and lifted Helen onto the stretcher.

Outside, rivers of red mud coursed along the track to the airstrip. It was impossible to keep dry and everyone was soaked to the skin in moments.

As Claire and Barry loaded Helen onto the plane, Brendan touched Bronte on the shoulder. 'There are no guarantees. The strip is a mess. We might not be able to get out. This front is stronger than was forecast.'

'Helen needs surgery or she'll die.' The bald words hung in the air between them.

'I understand, but I have to consider six lives, not just one.'

Bronte bit her lip. The decision rested with Brendan, and he had to consider everyone's safety. She sent up a prayer that they could get out of Nandana and started to walk up the plane steps. Rain lashed her, her hair stuck to her face and a pervading sense of doom overtook her.

Red-hot, searing pain pierced her belly. She doubled over, gripping the handrail, unable to move.

The baby.

Fear rushed through her, invading every part of her. Somehow she managed the last three steps into the plane.

The pain hit again, strong, fierce and terrifying. This time she felt a warm, thick wetness between her legs. Blood.

No! A voice screamed in her head. No, this couldn't be happening. She still had six weeks before her due date. She instinctively crossed her legs.

But an antepartum haemorrhage didn't care about dates or prematurity. It didn't care that at thirty-four weeks gestation her baby's lungs might not be mature enough to work without assistance. Didn't care that she was one thousand kilometres from a neonatal nursery. That Huon was nowhere close by and she was the only doctor.

The isolation of the outback rammed home loud and clear.

Now three lives hung in the balance.

The rain thundered against the plane. Everything was in the lap of the gods.

CHAPTER ELEVEN

SYDNEY HARBOUR SPARKLED blue through the famous seafood restaurant's window. Not a grain of red dirt to be seen. Huon listened to his medical colleagues talking about the merits of discussing routine folate intake to all women of childbearing age.

But his mind kept wandering to Muttawindi. Had Jack's test results come back? Would the old devil have gone to see Bronte about them?

Bronte.

He ran his hand through his hair and suddenly stopped midway. *Whenever you're worried about something or needing to do something you don't want to do, you run your hand through your hair.*

Bronte's words rang in his head. She'd noticed things about him he hadn't even noticed himself. She knew things about him no one else did. But there was no point going there. He couldn't love her. Not in the way she wanted. He couldn't love anyone in that all-encompassing way ever again.

And given time, she would understand that. She

would come to see that his decision was the right one. The only decision available to them.

His mobile phone vibrated. Claire's number came up on the display. He sighed inwardly. Claire was furious with him. He could understand that. He felt pretty lousy that he'd let things go so far with Bronte. He didn't need other people reminding him of his own shortcomings.

Claire had given him a verbal serve two nights ago. He loved his foster-mother dearly, but he really didn't want to have another conversation about Bronte. Not now anyway. He'd let the call go through to message bank.

He forced his concentration back to the discussion that surrounded him.

'Huon.' Jason Craig, a fellow doctor from Queensland, hailed him from across the room.

Huon walked towards him and shook his hand. 'Good to see you, Jason.'

'You, too. Listen, I've just been speaking to that gorgeous flight nurse of yours, Hayley Gaylard, on the phone. Muttawindi's trying to get hold of you. Hayley said something about a storm and a pregnant patient. Anyway, can you give her or Claire a ring now?'

A wave of concern rippled through Huon. 'Sure thing. Thanks, mate.' Perhaps Taylor Lewis had gone into labour. They probably couldn't find the file. He was certain it was on his desk.

He punched in Claire's number and waited for the phone to be answered.

'Huon, thank goodness.' Claire's usually firm and in-control voice, sounded fraught.

'What's up?' He was probably in trouble about the file that she'd wasted time looking for.

'It's Bronte.'

A chill traversed the length of his body, leaving a trail of dread. 'What about Bronte?'

Her voice trembled. 'She's had an antepartum haemorrhage.'

His stomach dropped to his knees and a roaring filled his ears. Not again. Surely life wasn't about to rip away another person he cared for? He gripped the phone tightly, his knuckles white. 'She's only thirty-four weeks pregnant.'

'I know that.' Claire paused. 'Huon, she's lost a lot of blood.'

His mouth went dry at the news. 'Where is she?'

'She's on her way to Adelaide.'

He heard the tears in Claire's voice and forced himself to concentrate on what he needed to know. 'What was the baby's condition when she left Broken Hill?'

'Distressed.'

'Hell, why didn't they do a Caesarean in Broken Hill?' He asked the question but he already knew the answer—he just didn't want to think about it. Bronte and the baby needed to be in a major hospital with intensive-care facilities. They could both die.

His heart twisted, sending immense pain into every corner of his body. His legs weakened. Bronte couldn't die. Bronte and the baby could not die. He wouldn't let that happen. He couldn't lose them.

He'd thought that if he pushed Bronte away he'd be immune to pain like this. God, how stupid had he been?

He'd hurt her badly, pushed her away, and left her alone. Now she was fighting for her life. Alone.

His chest tightened. It hurt to breathe.

'Huon.' Claire spoke slowly, as if speaking to a person who didn't understand English. 'Listen to your mother. Get on a plane, *now*, and go to Adelaide.'

But he didn't need to be told that. Every part of him knew he had to be with Bronte. He had to be by her side. She needed him.

He needed her.

Why had he thought he could keep her at arm's length? His heart belonged to her. And to the baby. It always had.

His mind raced. He had to get to Adelaide as soon as possible. He looked around at the crowded reception room. Who did he know in this room who had a plane?

Two hours later he ran up the stairs to the birthing suite at Flinders Medical Centre. Thoughts of death skittered across his brain, and bleakness entered his soul. What if he'd arrived too late?

He hated himself. He should have been there. He should have been in Muttawindi, not bloody Sydney. It should have been him accompanying Bronte on the flight to Adelaide, not Hayley.

Guilt ate into him. Thank God she'd had Hayley. And Claire. But he should have been with her. She would have been distraught with fear. She knew the possible outcomes of a bleed in pregnancy. The loss of the baby.

And he'd forced her to cope with all this on her own.

He rounded the corner of the unit and called out to the nurse. 'I need to see Bronte Hawkins, she's a doctor, but she's pregnant and a patient and…,' the incoherent words tumbled out, carrying his fear.

The young nurse looked at him with concern. 'Take a deep breath, sir. Are you a relative of Dr. Hawkins?'

'No, I'm not but—'

'I'm sorry, sir, but it's immediate family only.'

The nurse turned away.

'I don't think you understand, I'm a doctor too, Huon Morrison, and I work with her. I need to see her.'

The nurse turned back. 'I can take a message.'

Frustration surged inside him. He'd battled Sydney traffic, a raging electrical storm and a light plane trip to get here. No one was going to stop him from seeing her. 'You don't understand. I love her.'

He heard the words and recognised the truth. He realised he'd been fighting the truth from the moment he'd met her. His heart was inexorably entwined with hers.

'Pardon me?' Surprise lined the nurse's face.

'I said I love her. And I need to see her so I can tell her that.'

The nurse gently rested her hand on his arm. 'You might have to wait to tell her. Right now she's heavily sedated in Intensive Care.'

He gripped the reception desk. 'Is she all right?' The question sounded inane. By definition, people in Intensive Care were not all right.

'She's lost a lot of blood and they're worried about complications. The next forty-eight hours will be crucial, but you know that, Doctor.'

He bit his lip. Yeah, he knew that. A breath shuddered through his body. He was scared to ask the next question but knew he had to. 'And the baby?'

'The baby is in Neonatal Intensive Care.' The straightforward words simultaneously lessened and worsened his fears. 'Who would you like to see first?'

He desperately wanted to see Bronte. Hold her hand, tell her he loved her, but if he saw the baby first he could tell her about the baby. Give her a reason to fight. A reason to survive.

He turned and walked towards NICU. Autopilot took over as he struggled to function in the darkness that enveloped him. One foot followed the other.

Three hours ago he'd been so convinced that his life's plan of living alone was correct. Now he desperately wanted a wife and a baby so much that it hurt.

Now he might never have them.

The nurse walked him through to the baby. Huon rested his hands on the Perspex of the Humidicrib and stared at the tiny child.

Translucent. Fragile. Delicate.

It was hard to work out where the wires and drips stopped and the baby started.

'Dr Morrison?' A young intern put his hand out. 'I'm Kieran Hamilton, and I'm looking after Baby Hawkins.'

Huon dragged his eyes away from the baby. 'Resps are up.'

'Yes, they are. We're hoping with the oxygen that this little battler will find breathing less of a struggle. Due to the rapid delivery there wasn't time to administer anti-inflammatory drugs, but at thirty-four weeks we're not certain of how much value the lungs gain from them anyway.'

Kieran checked the oxygen levels. 'The next couple of hours will be crucial for your baby. We're hoping to see an improvement.'

Your baby. Huon didn't correct the intern. He wanted so much for this baby to be his. 'And if there's no improvement, you intubate and nurse in an open cot?'

'That's correct.' Kieran rested his hand on Huon's shoulder in a sympathetic gesture. 'Page me any time.'

Huon nodded his thanks and turned back to the baby. A desperate need to touch the tiny child filled him, bringing with it a rush of primal, gut-wrenching love.

He flattened his hands against the Humidicrib in a futile gesture to get closer. Tears pricked the backs of his eyes at the sheer miracle of a new life. A life that was struggling with every breath. He watched the tiny rib cage shudder up and down.

'Come on, little one. Your mummy loves you so much, and so do I.'

The nurse touched his arm. 'I'll take you to see Dr Hawkins now.'

He nodded, blew his nose, and walked to Intensive Care.

Huon was always amazed at how busy yet quiet Intensive Care was. The silence was punctuated only by the beeping machines and low voices.

Like the baby, Bronte lay with tubes and drips and wires attached to her. Her glorious hair, the hair he loved to bury his face in, rested like a dark veil against the white pillowslip.

Love and fear collided. His heart lurched. He sat down next to her and lifted her cool hand, cradling it between his own. 'Bronte, it's Huon.'

'She's sedated so you might not get much of a response at the moment.' The nurse smiled at him. 'But talk to her. Tell her what you told me, I'm sure she'll want to hear that.'

'It might be a bit late.' His voice trembled.

'She's stable at the moment, Doctor. We've passed the first hurdle.' The nurse tried to sound reassuring.

Huon sighed. 'What I mean is, she might not want to know. I've been a bit slow at realising it.'

She nodded in understanding. 'Love is one big risk, Doctor. But if you don't take the risk, you lose out on so much more.'

'I'm starting to realise that.'

'That's the first step. I'll leave the two of you alone.' She pulled the curtains closed behind her.

Where did he start? He rested his head on her hair and breathed in her scent. Somehow, even with all the surgical antiseptic and anaesthetic gases, her trade mark spicy scent lingered. He breathed deeper. He needed to be as close to her as possible.

He squeezed her hand. 'Bronte, you have a daughter. If she has half the fighting spirit of her mother, she'll pull through with flying colours.'

He watched the rise and fall of her chest and scanned her face for signs of recognition, but she slept soundly. He dragged in a breath. 'You've had me so scared I could hardly breathe. I thought I might lose you and the baby. I pulled in every favour I could and got here as fast as I could. I know it doesn't make up for me not being with you when you needed me most.'

His voice quavered. 'Please, wake up so I can tell you what a bloody idiot I've been. Please, wake up so I can tell you I love you.'

He leaned forward, his lips grazing hers. Willing her to wake up, willing her to respond to him. He needed her like he needed oxygen. But she slept on.

Pain. Sharp, hot, penetrating pain. Bronte stopped trying to move. Her mind struggled against the black fog, trying to make sense of what was happening. She remembered the flight, remembered her fear.

The baby.

She reached her hand down to her belly. Her fingertips touched flatness and a gauze dressing. Panic filled her. She tried to lift her head, use her voice.

'Bronte.'

She felt a hand over hers.

'It's all right. The baby's all right.'

Thank you. She whispered the words to herself. The baby was alive.

'She's a gorgeous little girl who's as beautiful as her mother.' The voice echoed in her head, trying to penetrate the thick fog that filled her brain.

Urgency filled her. 'I need to see her, hold her.' She tried to sit up but a spinning sensation pushed her backwards.

'You can, sweetheart. Very soon.' The deep timbre of the voice sounded clearer, familiar.

Huon's voice.

She fought the fog. It couldn't be Huon. He was in

Sydney. She was in Adelaide. She turned her head and tried to force her leaden eyes to open. The lids were so heavy they dragged against her efforts. 'Huon?'

'Yes, darling, it's me.' His ragged voice rasped the words.

She tried again and opened her eyes. Her vision blurred at first, then started to clear.

Huon leaned close to her, his penetrating blue eyes filled with worry. Deep crevasses of lines criss-crossed the black rings under his eyes. His hair spiked up as if he'd run his hand through it a thousand times.

The fog swirled in her head. He couldn't be real. She must be imagining this. She put her hand out and touched his cheek, rough stubble grazing her fingertips.

'You're here.' She heard the croaking disbelief in her voice.

'I am. I've been here two days.' He ran his hand through his hair. 'I should have never been away from you. I'm so sorry.'

'Two days?' She couldn't believe she'd lost two days. 'And Helen?'

'She's doing well. Better than you. You've been pretty ill and worrying us sick.'

'Us?' She grappled to think clearly.

'Me, your parents, Claire and the entire town.'

'My parents?' She tried to make sense of his words.

'They flew here. They love you.' He picked up her hand. 'I love you, too.'

Had she heard right? The words hammered in her head and she struggled to focus on his face. 'You love me?' Disbelief coloured her words.

'I love you with every part of me.' He brought her hand up to his face, resting it against his cheek. 'I've been such a fool. I had a gift in front of me and I threw it away.

'I'm *so* sorry. You have no idea how sorry I am. If I could turn back the clock, I would. I hope to make it up to you for the rest of your life.'

Her heart beat faster at the sincerity of his words. Words she'd so wanted to hear. And with his words, hope seeped into her, but she forced her brain to concentrate. She needed to know why he'd changed his mind, needed to be sure he really had. 'But you told me you didn't love me, that you couldn't give me what I wanted.'

'I've been a complete fool.' He sighed a ragged breath. 'I thought I couldn't give you what you wanted. And you were right about me living a half-life. After Ellen died I didn't want to risk loving anyone again. I didn't want to risk loving you.'

A ray of optimism shone inside her. He'd worked it out. He'd recognised what he'd been doing. 'And you pushed me away to try and keep your heart safe?'

He stroked her face and nodded. 'I did. But I made the biggest mistake of my life that night at the ball. I was scared. I was too scared to commit to you and the baby. I thought if I held back, I could never feel the pain of losing someone again.'

He blinked furiously. 'And it happened anyway. Two nights ago I thought you might die. The pain was so strong, so intense that I knew there and then I loved you.' His voice cracked. 'And all I could think of was I hadn't told you.'

Her heart surged with joy. Huon really loved her.

He'd been to hell and back while she'd lain in hospital. She wanted to hold him close to her, tell him it was all right, that she understood. But two IV drips and a monitor were in the way.

She squeezed his hand to reassure him. 'I'm here, Huon, and I'm fine.'

'And I'll give thanks for that every day of my life. I know I've hurt you. I know I've taken far too long to work this out, but I love you, Bronte. I think I've loved you from the moment I saw your cute behind sticking up in the air as you struggled with that worn-out case.'

She laughed, then gripped her belly where the stitches pulled. 'And to think I kicked that case when it had actually done me a big favour.'

He tucked her hair behind her ear. 'I love you with all my heart and I want to be part of your life. I want to be your lover, your husband and father to your gorgeous daughter. I can only hope you'll let me.'

She thought her chest would explode from happiness. He wanted to be with her. He'd put his fear aside and was looking to the future. A future with her and the baby.

She looked at his handsome face, etched with lines of worry and pain, and wanted so desperately to ease them away with loving hands. 'I'll let you love me and I'll love you straight back. I couldn't think of anything more wonderful than raising my daughter with you.'

'Will you marry me, Bronte?'

'Absolutely.' Elation filled her. Her life was just beginning. Muttawindi, Huon and a baby daughter. Bronte knew she'd finally found a true home.

EPILOGUE

MUTTAWINDI WAS DRESSED to party. Bunting hung in the streets, the band played and baby Georgina Claire, in a white lace dress, shrieked with delight when she saw her mother.

Bronte, radiant in a flowing ivory gown, smiled a smile of pure joy. The entire town and half the district had come for the wedding. An enormous white marquee lined the main street and the dance floor was, by request, half under cover, half under the stars.

It was hard to believe that four months ago everything had seemed so bleak. Today her new family surrounded her, as well as her old family and dear friends, who had all come to help her and Huon celebrate. Celebrate their love.

She looked over to her new husband of two hours. Looking drop-dead gorgeous in a tux, he was dancing with Mrs Nikvolski.

'Mrs Nikvolski always had a soft spot for Huon.' Claire's voice sounded in her ear.

Bronte laughed and turned towards Claire, who stood holding Georgina. 'Yes, she told me more than once how good he looked in a tux.'

'I doubt you have anything to worry about from that quarter. Huon's gazed seems permanently riveted to you.' Claire's face broke into a wide grin. 'And it shouldn't be any other way. Ron and I have to thank you for bringing Huon back into the real world. And for giving us a gorgeous granddaughter.'

Tears filmed Bronte's eyes. 'You raised a wonderful man, Claire. I should thank you.'

Claire sniffed. 'Off you go and dance with him, then. Georgie is fine with me, aren't you, sweetheart?'

Georgina blew a bubble, happy in her grandmother's arms.

Bronte gave a silent prayer of thanks for her good fortune. She had loving in-laws and a town that fought over the right to spend time with Georgina.

Georgie had shown a determined spirit from the start and had been able to come home to Muttawindi soon after she'd been born.

The joy of being a mother never ceased to amaze Bronte, the wonder of watching her daughter grow, the delight of holding her close and the extreme happiness of knowing that she had a loving father.

'Dr Morrison, are you ready to dance?' Huon's warm and loving hands snaked around her waist, pulling her back against him.

A surge of heat raced through her at his touch and she turned in his arms. 'I'm ready, Dr Morrison. Ready for a long, slow dance.'

His eyes darkened with desire and she thrilled that she could elicit this response from him.

He pulled her even closer, her body melding into his

in a perfect fit. 'Did I ever get around to telling you how beautiful you are in that dress?'

She laughed. 'Only about ten times.'

He ducked his head and nuzzled her neck. 'I'm looking forward to telling you how beautiful you are out of that dress.'

His voice, husky with emotion, sent ripples of white-hot sensation through her, making her ache with delicious anticipation. 'I'll hold you to that.'

'And I'll hold you and Georgie close to my heart for the rest of my life.' His lips grazed hers in a loving kiss, sealing his commitment to her.

And she kissed him right back.

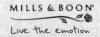

MILLS & BOON®

0706/03b

Live the emotion

_Medical romance™

BRIDE AT BAY HOSPITAL by *Meredith Webber*

Bad boy Sam Agostini left the bay thirteen years ago, leaving Nurse Megan Anstey broken-hearted. Now he is back, still devastatingly handsome, still undeniably charming, and a highly respected doctor. As Sam fights to make up to Megan for his past, new secrets start to bubble to the surface…

THE FLIGHT DOCTOR'S ENGAGEMENT
by *Laura Iding*

Air Rescue:
High flying doctors – High altitude medical drama

Flight doctor Zach Taylor is intrigued by his partner – fiery paramedic Jenna Reed. There is more to Jenna than meets the eye – and he is intrigued by her determination to rescue everyone and everything. Zach can see that it's Jenna herself who needs saving – his plan is to do exactly that and, hopefully, also win her heart!

IN HIS SPECIAL CARE by *Lucy Clark*

Despite being Mt Black Hospital's only full-time GP, Dr Claire Neilson always finds time for her patients. But Claire doesn't let anyone care for her…until the new specialist – incredibly handsome, enigmatic Dr Declan Silvermark arrives in the small Australian town and turns her carefully ordered world upside down…

On sale 4th August 2006

Available at WHSmith, Tesco, ASDA, Borders, Eason, Sainsbury's and most bookshops

www.millsandboon.co.uk

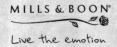

4 FREE

BOOKS AND A SURPRISE GIFT!

We would like to take this opportunity to thank you for reading this Mills & Boon® book by offering you the chance to take FOUR more specially selected titles from the Medical Romance™ series absolutely FREE! We're also making this offer to introduce you to the benefits of the Reader Service™—

- ★ **FREE home delivery**
- ★ **FREE gifts and competitions**
- ★ **FREE monthly Newsletter**
- ★ **Exclusive Reader Service offers**
- ★ **Books available before they're in the shops**

Accepting these FREE books and gift places you under no obligation to buy, you may cancel at any time, even after receiving your free shipment. Simply complete your details below and return the entire page to the address below. You don't even need a stamp!

YES! Please send me 4 free Medical Romance books and a surprise gift. I understand that unless you hear from me, I will receive 6 superb new titles every month for just £2.80 each, postage and packing free. I am under no obligation to purchase any books and may cancel my subscription at any time. The free books and gift will be mine to keep in any case.

M6ZED

Ms/Mrs/Miss/Mr ....Initials ....

BLOCK CAPITALS PLEASE

Surname ....

Address ....

....

....Postcode................................

Send this whole page to:
UK: FREEPOST CN81, Croydon, CR9 3WZ